FROSTBITE

DAVE JEFFERY

SEVERED PRESS
HOBART TASMANIA

FROSTBITE

Copyright © 2017 by Dave Jeffery
Copyright © 2017 by Severed Press

WWW.SEVEREDPRESS.COM

ISBN: 978-1-925597-75-2

CHAPTER ONE

The S'OAK pub was old school, a place of warped and pitted dark brown wood, perfumed by the pungent aroma of stale beer. The clientele were reflective of their environment: tired and weathered by the harsh experiences of inner city life.

Some of the regulars were sat at circular tables at odds with the uneven floor, or they were hunched over the bar - evenly spaced - but there was no room for conversation.

This was the place people came to mull over what once was: a place to keep secrets, or court regrets. Any talk when it did happen was basic, a veneer: the latest football match, the latest murder, whatever bullshit politicians were currently peddling.

The men and women were grizzled and hard-core, their perspectives … jaded. They gave off an air of warning to anyone who happened across their watering hole. Most knew to avoid it. Only those who were lost came here, and only those who did not want to be found stayed.

The licence-plaque above the bar said the owner went by the name of Hilary Adams. Not one of her patrons knew if this was her real name or not, and most of them didn't give a shit one way or the other.

Behind the bar, the sign's namesake stood scratching an emery board across her painted nails; her shrewd blue eyes surveying her dour domain the way a sated lion keeps watch over its pride. Her sallow cheeks bellowed as she whistled a non-tune. Cheap foundation - almost masking the lines about her face - caught the optic lights, making the surface of her cheeks shimmer like bacon grease.

Now in her late fifties, Adams had been alone for some time. Her husband had up and left ten years ago, never to be seen again. Her customers fancied she'd put rat poison in his tea one night before burying him in a dark and desolate place.

A slot machine played a merry tune in one corner of the room. Like her husband, the machine took more than it gave.

Tonight it pumped out a tenner in change, the coins tinkling in the collection tray almost mitigating the notion that any kind of promise it gave was as false as Adam's fingernails. There was only one winner in this place. She made sure of it.

The entrance door opened, and a stranger walked in. The murmur in the pub stopped; the newsreader's narrative from the big TV on the far wall filled in the silence.

The young woman was tall and so elegant she was instantly at odds with her surroundings. Her high cheekbones and deep brown eyes were only outshone by her lips which were full and painted with a deep strawberry gloss. She wore a light leather jacket, and sheer black leggings exaggerated her athletic physique. There was elegance in her movements, but something else was there too: confidence and a sense of dangerousness.

The woman stepped up and dragged a strand of blonde hair behind her right ear before putting a small, blue clutch-purse on a beer towel draped over the bar. She popped open the clasp and fished around looking for money.

Adams stopped her manicure and ambled over.

'You sure you're in the right place, love?'

Some of the men at the bar chuckled into their pints of heavy. Some made no attempt to stop gawping at the woman's arse.

'Huh?' the woman said as she looked up from her purse.

'The bistro and wine bar is on Sheriff Street,' Adams said. 'About a mile away?'

'Sounds nice,' the woman said with a smile. Her teeth were pearls under the bar lights. 'What bottled beers do you have?'

Adams studied the woman for a few moments then shrugged her shoulders. She stepped aside to reveal the fridge display behind her.

'I'll have a Beck's, please.'

Adams stooped for the beer. Her gait was stiff and awkward, her jeans tight on reed-thin legs. She came back and popped the bottle cap on the fixed opener screwed to the bar. She placed the beer by the purse and the woman reciprocated by slapping a note onto the counter.

It was a fifty.

'Ain't got change for that,' Adams said.

'No?' the woman said. The smile was back and her eyes were bright, playful. 'How about I let you keep it?'

Adams's brows arched and her mouth pulled into a tight, white hyphen.

'Ain't no one gives that kind of money away,' she said. 'What you want?'

'Information,' the woman said. She took a sip from her beer. After pulling a Smartphone from her jacket pocket, she presented it to Adams. There was an image on the screen. 'Do you know this man?'

'Cops aren't welcome here,' Adams said, not even looking at the phone.

The people around the bar sloped off to the tables as though they were somehow invisible.

'I'm not a cop.'

'Then who are you?'

'I'm just somebody looking for *someone*.' She tapped the screen of her phone. '*This* someone.'

'The drink's on the house,' Adams said turning away. 'Finish it and get lost.'

'Maybe if I added something to the fifty?' the woman said calmly.

Adams turned briskly, a retort already building at the back of her throat.

But when she saw the item lying on top of the fifty-pound note, any tirade she had primed was neutralised in an instant. Instead she looked at the woman who was now taking another draw from the beer bottle.

'He's upstairs,' Adams said cautiously.

***

The room isn't real, it is just a skewed memory of how things used to be; such is the nature of dreams.

In this dream-room Grant Hastings is cradling a baby, its tiny form dwarfed by his huge frame, his bulky forearms supporting swathes of linen that wriggles lazily under his touch.

There are sounds too: gurgles of contentment as the infant drifts off to sleep after its mid-morning feed.

A hand on his shoulder has him turning, and there is Renata, proud mother, wonderful wife, and she is smiling down at their child, and her expression speaks only of unconditional love. She snuggles her head against his bicep; her hair smells of wild cherry.

'Where did the time go?' he sighs.

'It wasn't time we lost, Grant,' she says without reproach. 'It was you.'

'I had to go,' he says. 'You know that. You can't turn away from duty.'

'And you can't stop time,' Jennifer says.

The room rotates like a cheap fairground attraction, the walls gathering speed until they are nothing more than a stomach lurching blur; the floor dropping away, and below there is the tangled canopy of a dark jungle. Renata and their baby have gone; the room replaced by a Chinook, and the child in his arms has swapped places with an M1 assault rifle.

The thud of chopper blades is loud and dense; the camouflaged faces of his companions are grim and taut with concentration.

'Where are my family?' Grant asks them.

One man, muscular frame made even more imposing by his bulky body armour, peers up at him with intense, blue eyes.

'Don't you remember? You had to leave them behind.'

'Why did I do that?' he screams above the rotor blades.

'Because it's who you are,' says his other companion, a slight black woman who brandished an assault rifle. Her face is screwed up in confusion as though this should be obvious to him.

'I loved them. I love them.'

'Sure you did,' the male marine says. 'But you loved the job more.'

There is a dawning, a realisation that all the things that he held dear have now fallen by the wayside; now they are only moments to be found in dreams.

When Grant Hastings wakes to loud thumps on the bedsit door, his pillow is as he always finds it these days: damp with sweat and tears of regret.

***

Hastings sat up in bed, the creaking springs of an aged mattress protesting at his movements. He kicked off the thin duvet and placed bare feet on the cold linoleum floor. Now upright, he allowed a coughing fit to clear away the dream.

Like the man who lodged there, the room was tired and unkempt. The stained, pale walls were adorned with cheap prints of ducks or flora; the furniture a mishmash of seventies kitsch and eighties monochrome. The kitchenette was a disaster area of pots and unwashed crockery; the small foldaway dining table was the only clear space on view.

The loud banging on the door helped stall Hastings' coughing bout. He cleared his throat enough to respond.

'Get lost, Hilary,' he grumbled. 'You got the rent. Now leave me be.'

'You got a visitor,' Adams said from behind the door.

'No one knows I'm here,' Grant said but he was now paying attention to the door. His right hand slid under the mattress beneath him, and it came out with a Glock 19.

'Well someone does,' Adams said. 'And they showed the sign you told me to look out for.'

Hastings paused, his eyes never leaving the door.

'Mr Hastings?' The woman's voice was articulate and well-spoken. 'I have something for you.'

There was a scuffling sound and Hastings' eyes fell to the bottom of the door where something was being pushed through into the room through the small gap between the scruffy wood and the linoleum.

Grant took a breath when he saw the brooch; the silver glimmered even in the low wattage bulb hanging from the cracked ceiling. The jewellery was fashioned into the image of a man tied to a tree, the figure pierced with several arrows.

Hastings nodded.

'What do you want?' Hastings said.

'Just a moment of your time. Nothing more.'

He thought this over. After a few moments he stood up and sought out his jeans and T-shirt. He pulled on the clothes, stowing the Glock in the waistband at the small of his back. Rubbing his eyes clear, he went to the door, his hand on the butt of the weapon.

He opened the door a crack and peered beyond. The woman was good on the eye, but he saw her body turned to the side, a pre-emptive stance he'd only seen in service personnel.

'Special forces?' he asked.

'Once upon a time,' she replied. 'You letting me in or what?'

'You got five minutes,' he said pulling open the door.

***

They sat opposite each other, Hastings on the bed, the woman at the dining table. Adams had gone back downstairs muttering something about hoping she still had a bar left to go back to while she'd been playing handmaid.

'So, who are you?' he said.

'Grace Appleby. My father is Marcus Appleby.'

'I'm not interested in your family tree,' he said. 'Why are you here?'

'My father *is* the reason I'm here.'

'Military?'

'Anthropology – he's a professor working out of the Museum of Natural History.'

Hastings gave her a 'so what' face. She continued with a wry smile; her eyes glazing as she recalled his resume.

'Grant Hastings, sergeant, 42nd Commando, three tours Afghanistan, two tours Iraq, countless off grid excursions into Syria; commander of *'The Sebs'*, an elite black ops extraction team named after Saint Sebastian.' She held up the brooch. 'Patron saint of soldiers. And now a password to get your attention.'

Hastings shrugged.

'So you know about me. What you want, a medal?'

Grace looked about her.

'What happened to you?'

'I retired.'

'I heard it was more than that,' she said as her eyes found him again.

'Then why you asking?' He made no attempt to temper his irritation.

'Because we heard you were the best,' she said frankly.

'I was the best,' he's sighed. 'Now I'm…'

'Fucked?' she offered.

'Retired. I might have mentioned that already.'

'And how's that working out for you?' she said pointedly.

'It's fine,' he said, fidgeting a little.

'Well, I can see it's paying dividends.'

'Some things can't be bought,' he said.

'Most things can. Even peace of mind,' she said. 'Being the best costs, right?'

'You're trying my patience,' he snapped. 'That stunt with the trinket bought you five minutes, and that time's almost up. It's only the fact you were able to find me that's keeping me interested.'

'We need your services,' she said quickly.

'Keep up with the story, lady. I don't do that shit anymore.'

'You don't know what "shit" we want you to do,' she said. 'All my father wants is an opportunity to present you with a business deal. That's all. And all I'm asking now is that you come with me, and listen to what he has to say. Take the deal, don't take the deal, you get five grand no matter what. I'll even drop you back at this shit hole afterwards. What do you say?'

Hastings stared at her, face impassive. The seconds ticked out; outside the window a car horn blared in the distance.

'Okay,' he said eventually. 'Where we going? Museum?'

'No. The park. He likes to feed the ducks,' she said glancing down at Hastings' bare feet. 'You got any shoes?'

***

Hastings followed Grace outside where a black SUV waited on the street, its tinted windows adding to the mystique.

A large man with a bald head and sunglasses leaned against the back door, arms crossed, the material of his grey suit barely able to contain the muscle beneath.

He gave Hastings a cursory nod before opening the door. Hastings paused to look inside the car and then climbed in.

Grace joined him on the opposite side.

'Cofton Park, Johns,' she said to the big man who got behind the wheel.

'You got it,' Johns said, and pulled the car away from the kerb.

Hastings placed his forehead on the window and watched the tinted world go by. His brown eyes ached; he rubbed his dark hair, still damp from the quick swill he'd had prior to leaving his lodgings. He allowed his finger to stop at his chin, where it scratched at a three-day growth of beard.

'You always fidget this much?' Grace asked.

'Only when I'm awake.'

Grace leaned forwards and opened a compartment between them where a selection of shots nestled in a small mini-bar.

'Think this'll help?' she said.

'No,' he said. But he helped himself all the same.

CHAPTER TWO

Johns parked the car outside the park gates. The drive through the city had taken fifteen minutes. The traffic was light, most people were at their desks or behind retail counters, and the only obstacles had been traffic lights and contraflows. It gave Hastings time to finish most of the minibar; giving him enough of a buzz to dull dreams of guilt and regret.

Contrary to what most who didn't know him would have thought, Hastings wasn't booze-dependent. He just enjoyed drinking. But there were periods of time when he drank more than others. Anniversaries and birthdays of either his wife or his daughter were always mourned with enough alcohol to pickle the average cadaver. In between such times, he spent the days booze free, needing the bright pangs of remorse to make their mark on the man he'd become. This was because on most days he felt as though he deserved the pain such things brought to him.

This was his penance for being selfish. And just like the outcomes of his self-absorbed existence, Hastings embraced it, owned it, the last act of atonement in a world he had managed to turn to shit.

'You coming or what?'

Hasting looked up and saw Grace peering at him through the open door of the vehicle. Her hair hung down like the gilded locks of a fairy tale princess, and Hastings considered the possibility that she was quite possibly one of the most beautiful women he'd ever seen.

Shit, he thought. *Maybe that last shot of vodka was pushing it too far*. He grabbed the car door and opened it, standing as the sunlight dazzled his eyes. Grace came to him and placed a hand lightly on his elbow, steering him forwards.

Johns stayed with the car, his purpose fulfilled it seemed, and Hastings walked with Grace through the wide expanse of green lawns and ornate pathways. Mums watched as their pre-school kids played on swings and climbing frames; OAPs strolled alongside the lake at the centre of the park where ducks cut V shapes into the dirty brown water.

As they passed by the play area, Hastings found his eyes flitting to the climbing frames where two young girls were laughing breathlessly as they chased each other.

'You miss it, I guess?' Grace said.

'I don't know you,' he said. 'I sure as hell don't know you enough to talk about *that*. We clear?'

'Sure.' It was a statement, nothing more. 'My father is up ahead.'

'Where?' he said.

She pointed towards the lake where one of the many benches located about the park was facing the water. A figure sat with ducks at their feet, the birds scrabbling for chunks of bread.

As they neared, the man on the bench looked up at them. Hastings estimated he was in his early sixties but still had a generous mop of grey-white hair that blended with a neatly trimmed beard. His grey eyes were behind rectangular, gold-framed glasses. He stood up and the movement was smooth, his trim figure demonstrating a man who knew the benefits of keeping in shape.

'Mr Hastings,' Appleby said offering his hand, the waxed, green Barbour jacket the older man wore creaked at the movement.

'Professor,' Hastings acknowledged taking the hand and pumping it twice. 'I thought we'd be meeting somewhere more...'

'Stuffy?' Appleby said with a small chuckle. 'I spent eight years at Oxford University's Museum of Natural History; that's enough stuffiness for any grounded anthropologist. I'm very much a hands-on scientist.'

'I heard this isn't about science,' Hastings said.

Appleby gestured for the Hastings to sit down beside him. Grace walked down to the edge of the lake and stood staring out across the water.

Hastings went to sit but found an object preventing him from doing so - a black briefcase on the bench's beech wood slats.

'What's that?' he said.

'Your fee for this little chat,' Appleby said. 'No doubt Grace told you the arrangement.'

'Yeah,' Hastings said as he picked up the case. He sat back down and placed the briefcase at his feet. 'I ain't used to people sticking to the deal.'

'Quite,' Appleby said. He watched Grace squat and throw rogue pieces of discarded bread to the ducks who had now migrated back to the bank.

'So why am I here?' Hastings said.

'My son is missing.'

Appleby's frankness caught Hastings off guard. He took a moment for the professor's comment to sink in.

'Ain't that a job for the police?' he said.

'That won't do any good,' Appleby said. 'He's abroad.'

'I hear they got police abroad.'

'It's not that kind of *missing*.'

'Go on.'

'His name is Michael and he's thirty-nine years old,' he said softly. 'A brilliant scientist. Father of my two grandchildren. You're a father too are you not?'

'That's not up for discussion.'

'I understand. I merely meant that you know what it is like to lose your family.'

Hastings sat back in his seat, but he was tense. He was prepared to fight anything but a past he'd helped to destroy.

'Will you help me, Mr Hastings?' Appleby said. 'I'm a man of means, but even I have my limits.'

'Well, I can't dispute that,' Hastings said. 'I won't ask how the hell you found me.'

'Ask, and I'll tell you,' Appleby said bluntly. 'But it involved lots of money and calling in many favours.'

'Who says money can't get you anything you want?' Hastings said.

'Well,' Appleby said with emphasis, 'that adage still remains to be seen.'

'Where is he?' Hastings said. 'Your son.'

'Nepal,' Appleby said. 'The Annapurna Range.'

'You mean the *Himalayas*?' Hastings said.

'Yes.'

'What the hell is he doing there?'

'That's altogether a different story,' Appleby said.

'The five grand at my feet says I got time to hear it,' Hastings replied.

'He was on expedition,' Appleby said.

'There ain't nothing but mountains, right?'

'There's a lot more than that.' Appleby smiled. 'The foothills of Machapuchare have botanical significance. And then of course there is the wildlife.'

Appleby paused as he saw disinterest in Hastings' eyes.

'So he was going to Machapuchare,' Hastings said. 'What happened?'

'He went into the mountain with his team four days ago. Was meant to stay in touch via satellite link up. Once a day. Last I heard from him was two days ago.'

'What are the local authorities saying?'

'This is the crux of the matter, Mr Hastings. They don't know he's there.'

'Maybe you should *tell* them?'

'Another sticking point,' Appleby said. 'The mountain is considered sacred, and an ascent is prohibited by law.'

'So how did he get near it?'

'The nearest city is Pokhara. It's the second biggest city in Nepal and considered the country's tourist capital,' Appleby said. He sounded as though he was reading from a tourist guide. 'Michael's team just acted as though they were Trekkers heading for the lower valleys which are still legally accessible.'

'So he was going *off piste*?'

Appleby nodded.

'Care to tell me what he was doing there?'

Appleby considered this for a moment.

'Do you believe in God, Mr Hastings?'

'I believe in anyone who delivers on a deal,' Hastings said.

'Indeed,' Appleby said. 'People are strange as *The Doors* once said. They believe in spiritual redemption yet require physical evidence before they can dispel things traditionally labelled as myth or legend.'

'What things?' Hastings said. 'Why was your son on that mountain?'

'He was looking for the Yeti, Mr Hastings,' Appleby replied. 'And I fear he may have found it.'

'Okay, Professor, I think that's my cue to leave.'

Hastings sat forward on the bench, his intention to stand, taking the money, and leaving behind the madness of Appleby's incredible statement.

'I'm very serious,' the professor said. His stern face reinforced his comment.

'You're talking about monsters used to scare kids. I ain't seeing any serious in that.'

'I'm talking anthropological wonders that have been seen roaming the Himalayas for centuries. And seen by many,' Appleby said with mild irritation.

'Not only locals but respected scientists and climbers too. Men of *distinction*.'

'So why isn't this stuff all over the news?'

'Doubters like yourself see a lack of consistent evidence as proof these incredible creatures cannot exist outside the imagination,' Appleby said. 'But I say it merely shows how elusive and intelligent they are. Michael certainly believes it. As do I. Enough to fund the expedition.'

Hastings looked from the brevity in Appleby's eyes to Grace who was standing watching them both, arms crossed. The lake shimmered in the noon sun, giving radiance to her tight, athletic frame. As he gazed upon her, Hastings tried to ignore the fact it had been some time since he'd had sex. He quashed the idea that Grace would be a nice way to end his period of celibacy and turned back to Appleby, who continued to regard him.

'I understand your scepticism,' he said. 'But this proposition is founded in business, not science. Whether you believe any of this or not, the fact remains that my son is missing, and I want him found. For that I will give you sixty thousand pounds on top of the money in that case – irrespective of the outcome. So, I ask you again, Mr Hastings: will you help us?'

Hastings considered this, and to anyone looking in, he would have appeared calm and considered. In truth, his mind raced. Gut instinct said to pull away from the deal, take the five grand,, and chalk it up to some well overdue good fortune. This, however, short lived. His recent dream was influencing his decision, a siren that called out to him, the means to put something right was now presenting itself in all its glittering, mesmerising glory. Sixty-grand was a huge sum, and Hastings calculated that even though he'd not been able to provide his daughter with physical and emotional support during her time on the earth, he could sure as hell make sure she was secure. This was what he did best after all, protect his own, the gears of war belonged inside a machine of his making, he steered it, fuelled it. The trust fund he intended to set up for his daughter's future was his way of delivering the goods, both as a father and a man. Though there were times when he questioned if he ever qualified for either of these labels.

But he could try, and it was this that finally had him nodded an accord.

'Hell,' he sighed. 'It's your money, Professor.'

'Thank you,' Appleby said, sounding relieved.

'Yeah,' Hastings said. 'But if you've really done your homework, you'll know I don't work alone.'

'Will you call them?' Appleby said. Hastings shook his head.

'Nah,' Hastings said. 'These are the kind of people you only get on board in person.'

CHAPTER THREE

Hastings stood and watched the garage across the street. It was a squat unit built within the shell of two terraced houses, knocked through to make a large bay. There was a small car park out front and, to the left of the bay, a door painted a hideous green. Hastings checked the traffic and crossed over the road, heading for the door which he pushed open, wincing at the shrill automated bleep announcing his arrival.

The reception was compact and stank of engine oil. A few moth-eaten chairs and a rickety coffee table were all that was on offer to waiting customers. The walls were plastered with dog-eared posters of high performance cars, and advertising for various vehicle components.

The man behind the counter was small with a round, ruddy face. Hastings got the impression that the e-cigarette clamped between the guy's cyanosed lips was a stopgap until he got outside and away from the "no naked flames" sign on the wall.

Hastings stepped up to the counter and the guy eyeballed him.

'Can I help you?' The name badge on the overall was askew and said he was Alan Carter.

'Looking for Patrick Vine,' Hastings said. 'He works here?'

'Depends on what your definition of work is,' Carter said. 'Who's asking?'

'I'm a friend of his.'

'One of his army pals?'

'No.'

'You're a shit liar, my friend,' Carter grinned and sucked on the e-cigarette. 'But what do I care? He's in the back. Don't keep him long. He's paid by the hour.'

'Thanks,' Hastings said, and went to the left of the counter where a door opened out into the workshop.

He stepped into the work bay where a Ford Focus was jacked up on the ramp. Underneath the vehicle stood an imposing figure of a man well over six feet tall, stretching to accommodate the wrench working on the chassis overhead.

An iPhone rested on a stack of tyres, its Bluetooth connected to speakers secured to the high walls where Roxette's JOYRIDE pumped out at full pelt. Hastings stepped up to the device and hit the pause button. The sudden silence was shocking, and the man underneath the car turned to identify what was going on. When he saw Hastings, he shook his head in disbelief.

'Only you'd have the nerve to turn that off,' he said, his overalls a mixture of taut material and grease-streaks.

'Only you'd have the nerve to listen to that shit, Vine,' Hastings said with a grin. 'Fucking Roxette?'

'Best band on the planet and you know it,' Vine said. He climbed from the pit and placed the wrench on the pile of tyres before wiping his greasy hands on a cloth just as dirty. 'Thought we were through.'

'So did I.' Hastings offered his hand. Vine took hold of it and pumped his arm a few times. The grin on his face was infectious and Hastings caught it.

'What changed?'

'The usual,' Hastings said. 'Want in?'

'Not sure,' Vine said. 'Got a good thing going here.'

'Sixty thousand,' Hastings said. 'Locate and rescue. Low combat risk.'

Vine looked over at Carter who was peering at them through the open doorway.

'Hey, Al,' he called.

'What is it Pat?'

'I quit,' Vine said, picking up his iPhone.

***

The metal ladder was perched precariously, its legs straddling an uneven lawn and a cluster of shrubs. The aluminium frame was alive with rattling sounds, the rungs bouncing against the plastic sills as its owner busied themselves cleaning the panes of leaded glass, the suds from a window rag arching in the air like fat snowflakes that slapped heavily against the tarmac driveway.

Hasting watched the window cleaner reach out to the next window without any apparent concern for their safety. But that was what made Hayley Knowles so dangerous. Vine stood beside him, big hands jammed into the pockets of his greased overalls.

'You're gonna send that ladder east as you go west if you ain't careful, Knowles!' Vine called.

If Knowles was startled, she didn't show it. Instead, she dropped the rag into the bucket hanging on the top rung and turned to look down at them with her big brown eyes. She had her hair pulled back from her face and rammed underneath a red baseball cap. Her ebony skin glistened with sweat.

'Well fuck me sideways,' she said. Her smile was genuine enough but there was uncertainty in her voice. 'Who died?'

'We all did,' Vine said with a grin. 'And this is Heaven.'

'Shit,' Knowles said descending the ladder. 'Then it wasn't worth the wait getting here.'

She came over to them, and they all embraced. It was natural, a thing they had done countless times. But it had been a while since the last time. The last time they'd been saying goodbye.

'Thought we weren't doing this again,' Knowles said.

'Thought we wouldn't,' Hastings admitted. 'But I got a gig that is less of a risk than seeing you up that ladder for another few years.'

'Go on,' she said, pulling off her cap and allowing her dreads to tumble over her shoulders.

'Not here,' Hastings said looking about him.

'What you scared of?' she said. 'Thought this was low risk?'

'Old habits, right?' he said.

'Fuck, yeah,' she said with a smile.

***

'You're fucking kidding me, right?'

Knowles scowled over the brim of a huge Costa coffee cup. About them the cafe was bustling with late afternoon patrons - mums corralling their boisterous kids, low-brow businessmen huddled over cheese Panini and espresso.

'I know it sounds crazy ...' Hastings began, but his incredulous counterpart interjected.

'Sounds crazy?' she said. 'It is crazy. Fucking *Yeti* for Christ' sake? Think I'm best stuck up a ladder slopping suds on windows. Fucking Yeti!'

A few people looked over at their table.

'Will you keep it down?' Hastings said.

'What's the problem?' Knowles scoffed. 'You think people might hear the crazy bullshit you're peddling?'

But it was Vine who replied.

'Maybe we're just not used to your articulate language anymore,' he grinned.

'Perhaps you could use that soapy water on that mouth of yours.'

She ruffled her brow, and her eyes narrowed for a few seconds. Her pursed lips trembled before the laughter started. Hastings and Vine joined in, and the tension between them was diffused for the moment at least.

As their laughter died down, Hastings leaned forward.

'You're looking two weeks, tops,' he said. 'We go with Appleby and look for his son. The other stuff is garbage. You know it; we know it. But its sixty grand apiece, either way.'

'If this guy believes in monsters,' Knowles said, 'how do we know he ain't dreaming up the money?'

'Because he's already put it into a private offshore account set up in our names,' Hastings said. 'And I've already got the account password.'

'Tested it?' she asked.

'What do you think?'

'I think I'm spending two weeks in Nepal,' she smiled.

***

Johns came to pick up Hastings and the others later that evening. Vine and Knowles had rendezvoused at the S'OAK and were entertaining two pints of lager when Hastings came downstairs with a black hold-all.

Adams was watching him intently as he came into the bar. He met her gaze and put the hold-all on the counter.

'This is my retainer for keeping the room,' he said. 'We got a deal?'

She came to the hold-all and pulled the zipper back a few inches before peering inside. Her face remained neutral, but her eyebrows quivered slightly.

She closed the bag and looked at him.

'It's a deal,' she said, and dragged the hold-all behind the bar with the fervour of a moray eel yanking its prey into its dark, subterranean lair.

Johns came through the main doors as Vine was draining his glass.

Knowles' shrewd eyes scrutinised the newcomer.

'You ready?' Johns said to Hastings.

'Er, hello. People standing here,' Knowles said, her tone sardonic. 'Your manners are about as shit as your fucking suit.'

Johns gave her a token glance before addressing Hastings again.

'This foul-mouthed retard with you?' Johns said.

'Motherfucker!' Knowles spat.

Hastings managed to block her as she went for Johns. Vine stepped up to add support as the woman fought to get past them both.

'You watch your mouth,' Vine growled at Johns. 'Or you'll find my boot in it.'

But Johns merely smirked, unimpressed by the threat. Vine turned his attention to Knowles who was being placated by Hastings.

'Look,' Hastings said once he was sure the heat had gone out of Knowles. 'We're all on the same payroll. Let's play nice, okay?'

'Works for me,' Johns said.

'Once this is done, you and me are going to have a discussion,' Knowles said to Johns.

'You and me both,' Vine said to Knowles.

'I'm not usually up for a threesome,' she said, 'but in this case I'll make an exception.'

'Let's just concentrate on the mission,' Hastings said firmly. 'We got a missing person. It's time to start getting focused, okay?'

His tone was no-nonsense. Vine and Knowles immediately stood down as Johns nodded and headed for the exit.

'Good,' Hastings said as he watched the big man leave. 'Let's go to work.'

***

Johns drove them out of the city in the black SUV. Knowles was sat between her two companions and scowled at their driver for what seemed like most of the journey.

Hastings looked out of window and watched the houses and high rises give way to expanses of fields made yellow with rape or quilted brown and green farmlands.

'Where the hell you taking us, Johns?' Vine said as the SUV came off the main road and the Tarmac shrivelled down to a dirt track that meandered off into thick woodland.

'To the rendezvous point,' the big man said. The chassis compensated for the rough terrain, but the SUV's occupants still bounced around in their seats.

'Fuck me,' Knowles said. 'You trying to kill us before we get there?'

'We got a small window,' Johns said.

'For what?' Hastings asked.

'To get airborne,' Johns replied.

Hastings was about to ask for some clarity when the woodlands suddenly gave way to a large expanse. There were fields either side of a tract of grey concrete stretching out both east and west. A Gulfstream G550 private jet was taxiing on the runway, its white fuselage stark against the backdrop of trees.

'A fucking airstrip?' Knowles said in disbelief. 'Out here?'

'I guess professors get well paid,' Hastings said, though he didn't sound as though he believed it.

'This professor does,' Johns said. 'He's like no other.'

'So I heard, Vine said.

'Meaning what?' Johns said as he pulled over on the side of the runway. He parked between a grey Bentley and a pristine transit van. The Bentley's number plate read PROF ONE.

'Meaning not many people would go helping out someone spouting the kind of shit that guy is shovelling,' Knowles said.

'You aren't exactly *helping* anyone out are you?' Johns said as he turned off the engine. 'You're being paid. So, I guess that "shit" comes with the brief.'

'Well, we agree on something at last,' Knowles said. 'Admit you're a dickhead, and it'll be two for two.'

Johns surprised them all by smiling.

'You're funny,' he said. 'Maybe I won't kill you once this is all over.'

There may have been a smile on his lips, but the gleam in his eye was cold and harsh.

'We agreed to a cease fire,' Hastings reminded them. 'So stow it. Now.'

Silence came over them. But it was begrudging.

Johns climbed from the car as Hastings caught movement outside. He could see Appleby and Grace stepping out of the Bentley.

Vine whistled as he saw Grace's hair tousled by the wind.

'Hell, the view just got better,' he said leaning across Hastings for a better look. 'Who's the filly?'

'You got more chance of getting it on with Johns,' Knowles laughed.

'Hey,' Vine said appearing genuinely hurt. 'I got what it takes to pull a classy bird.'

'That you can say "classy" and "bird" in the same sentence tells me why you live a lonely life, mister,' Knowles chuckled.

'Could be worse,' Vine muttered. 'I could be shacked up with you.'

'Now you're scaring me,' she said flatly. 'Seriously. Never say that again.'

Vine laughed as he popped the door and threw it open. He shuffled outside, Knowles following him.

'Welcome, welcome,' Appleby said, stepping up to them and offering his hand. He was wearing khaki trousers and a plaid shirt. A green body warmer completed his outfit. The clothing looked packet-fresh. Grace still wore her leather jacket over black combat pants and boots. The wind bustled into them, and Appleby had to raise his voice to be heard.

'We got gear on the plane,' Appleby said. 'Weatherproof clothing and all that. We get the rest of our kit when we get to Nepal.'

'You're coming along too?' Hastings said.

'Of course,' Appleby said as though anything other than this would be inconceivable. 'Michael is my son. And Grace's brother.'

'We work alone,' Hastings said.

'And I will not interfere in the course of your work,' Appleby said. 'You have my word on that. But you must understand the terms of your employment, Mr Hastings. And they are laid out before you. You can still walk away if they are not to your liking.'

Hastings glanced to Vine and Knowles who merely shrugged their shoulders.

'Your call, chief,' Vine said.

Hastings thought it over, and then nodded to Appleby.

'Okay,' he said. 'But I call the shots if we run into trouble. And that means everyone,' he said eyeballing Johns and Grace. 'Agreed?'

'Most certainly,' Appleby said. Grace appeared nonplussed and difficult to read. Johns gave out his trademark smirk.

'If such circumstances arise we have an agreement,' the professor said to make it clear to all. 'Now shall we get on board? We're on a schedule after all.'

Without another word he made for the plane, Grace at his side. Johns followed on behind.

'How can you call the shots if we get into trouble if there isn't going to *be* any trouble?' Knowles asked. 'Weren't you the one who specifically said there was going to be a distinct absence of trouble on this trip? If not, you've got one hell of a fucking roaming around town.'

'Ah, stow it, Knowles,' Vine said. 'You know there's always trouble. It follows us around like a hungry mutt. Isn't that right, chief?'

Hastings watched as Grace stopped to look back at them. He left the wind to answer Vine's question.

CHAPTER FOUR

The flight to Nepal took almost nine hours, the G550 having the capacity to travel the four and a half thousand-mile trip without a refuel. During this time, Hastings and his team relaxed on beige leather sofas or bucket seats, playing cards or cat napping.

Throughout the flight, Hastings observed Appleby and his daughter, the close knit nature of family relationships as they sat opposite each other; the fold down table separating them strewn with maps and satellite images of the Annapurna region. Their discussions were quiet and considered. Hastings found himself admiring them both; their ability to remain focused on the task at hand, given what they had the potential to lose, was not a thing he found common in people. He figured that Grace had acquired some of this through time served, but Hastings knew all too well such things were not always ironed out through training and combat experience.

He knew this because of his own sense of loss. A daughter he barely knew and an estranged wife who knew him a little too much. Combat did things to people. Only the fucking MOD failed to recognise it. Too much come back – not enough mitigation.

Hastings sat back in his seat and sighed. Sometimes he just wished things had turned out differently; turned out better. Part of him liked to think that his current situation had nothing to do with him; that fate had just come along and decided to take a dump on his life. Whenever he tried to embrace this as an idea, the boot of reality kicked its way through and dragged him outside his castle of delusion into the stark, terrifying light of the obvious: he'd made some bad calls, and his life was now living with the echoes.

Renata always told him she saw distance in his eyes. Even in the early days when they had made love on the roof of the high rise they'd shared when first courting, the stars overhead, and their naked bodies marked by the skeletal shadows of communications antennae. He's always denied her statements but inside it left him uncomfortable, like a scab that isn't quite ready to be pulled off a healing wound. She was right though. He struggled to let go. He suspected that Vine and Knowles were the same but he never asked them. Plenty who specialised in covert ops knew the score; it was not a job, saving lives was a life in itself, no switching off from it, no compartmentalising it – parking it up – as you took leave and tried to play happy families as the screams and gurgles of the dying followed you home. Too many became addicted to the game, and Hastings had been a great player.

He rubbed a hand across his face and turned onto his side, the leather sofa squeaking at the movement. He closed his eyes and hoped that he could take a break from attrition only to find that, just like the muttered words of the dying, it was to follow him into the darkness.

***

When the jet landed at Pokhara airport, it taxied to a small hanger where the scream of the engines fell like the breath of a sated infant. Appleby, who had pretty much been awake for the entire flight, appeared fresh and motivated, standing as soon as the plane had stopped. He reached beneath his seat and pulled from it a small briefcase, not dissimilar to that he'd given to Hastings in the park. He passed this to Johns.

'Make sure this goes to our contact in air traffic control,' Appleby said. He caught Hastings looking at the case. 'Pokhara is for domestic flights; nearest international airport is over five hundred kilometres away at Kathmandu,' he explained. 'I don't know about you but, while I enjoy a brisk walk, that kind of journey fails to inspire.'

Johns took the case as the aircrew, a male with a black moustache and a female with short brown hair, came from the cockpit and released the door. Grace went to them.

'Keep the plane here,' she said to the pilots. 'We have sanction to berth it in this hanger for as long as necessary. You'll be left in peace. We've made sure of it.'

The aircrew nodded and stood aside once they'd released the steps leading down to the tarmac.

Appleby turned to Hastings and his team. Johns and Grace alighted down the steps and the professor extended his hand towards the exit.

'Welcome to Nepal,' he said with a weary smile.

***

They ate in a restaurant in Pokhara city. The dining area was sectioned off by squared brick pillars, and overhead, thick beams of deep brown timber gave off a pungent aroma of smoked pine. Behind a rack of vertical bamboo slats, the serving counter was a place of steam and noise, the kitchen staff buzzing around and chattering excitedly. The whole venue had a warm and welcoming feel to it, and Hastings and the others settled down to their meal with a cautious yet contented refrain.

About them the patrons were made up of locals and tourists who were using the city as a base before heading off on organised treks into the Annapurna Sanctuary. It was getting late in the season, and most of the Trekkers at this point were ardent and experienced, not needing a guide for the lower slopes.

Their meals arrived and consisted of Dal Bhat, a serving of rice and grain with lentils accompanied by curried fish and meat dishes, yogurts, chutneys, and roti. Appleby ate thukpa, a hot noodle soup that was more in keeping with the Kathmandu region. They all ate the sweet crispy bagels known locally as Sel Roti.

Knowles sat back in her seat and let out a long burp.

'Shit that was nice,' she said, patting her non-existent stomach. 'Think I'll come back here.'

'Yeah,' Vine said with a smile. 'Wonder if they deliver?'

Hastings looked at the tourists sitting around them; many wore hiking boots and their cagoules were draped on the back of their chairs.

'I know that face,' Vine said. 'That's a *thinking* face.'

'Just working out our next move,' Hastings said. He looked at Appleby. 'Unless you got something in play?'

'I'm handing this over to you,' Appleby said as he held up his hands. 'I can tap into local resources up to a point - travel, equipment and the like. From here we are in your hands.'

'Then I'll need to know a few things,' Hastings said. 'Michael's last known co-ordinates and the routes that may take us nearby. What was the stuff you were looking at on the plane?'

'The co-ordinates are *twenty-eight degrees, twenty-nine minutes, 42 seconds north and thirty-eight degrees, fifty-six minutes and fifty seconds east*,' Grace said without thought. She had put her hair up into a bun, exposing her long pale neck where a slim, gold chain ended with a heart-shaped locket. Her eyes flitted across Hastings' face before settling on a table filled with locals engaged in jovial banter. 'That puts Michael at an altitude well over five thousand metres.'

'What does that mean?' Vine said.

'It means he's in the cold stuff,' Johns said.

'And we'll all be needing regular Diamox from this point on,' Appleby said. 'Altitude sickness is a silent killer.'

'Beats me why you guys couldn't come up with a plan of your own,' Vine said. 'You got military experience and the financial muscle to back it up.'

'We all have our areas of expertise, Mr Vine,' Appleby said. 'Even in the military as I am often told.' He gave Grace a playful nudge with his elbow. She smiled and looked down at her empty plate.

'Money gives you access to that and, by all accounts, I now have access to the best,' Appleby continued.

'Still don't get it,' Knowles said. 'A paid guide could've taken you where you need to go. *And* given you alternative routes.'

'You trying to talk us out of a job, Vine?' Hastings said.

'You might think that,' Grace interjected. 'But some things go deeper than money, right, Hastings?'

He scanned her face looking for spite but did not find it there. 'I think that way,' he said.

'And so do the people around here,' Appleby said. 'Yes, officials will turn a blind eye to certain types of, shall we say, *traffic*? But some things are strictly off limits.'

'Like the mountain?' Knowles said.

'Indeed,' Appleby replied. 'Machapuchare. It has twin peaks and is known as 'fish tail'. The locals believe that it is a sacred place; the seat of the Hindu god Shiva.'

'Destroyer of the World,' Knowles said.

'Why yes,' Appleby said in surprise. 'The mountain has never been climbed to its summit. Wilfred and Cox climbed to within two thousand feet of the top because of an agreement they made not to set foot on the summit. That was in 1957. The mountain has been totally out of bounds for climbers since that time.'

'So what is the penalty for breaching the agreement?' Vine asked.

'A huge fine and deportation,' Grace said. 'With no chance of ever getting back into the country again.'

'I see,' Hastings said taking a sip from his coffee cup. 'I guess that's enough of a deterrent for climbers. What about the guides who might want to help them?'

'The guides simply *won't* help them, Mr Hastings,' Appleby explained. 'Because they are terrified of the potential consequences.'

'From the law?' Hastings said.

'No,' Appleby said and there was a familiar gleam back in his eyes. 'From something that transcends trivial rules of man.'

'Oh, man,' Knowles sighed. 'You talking about that Yeti shit again?'

Appleby looked at her, and his face was grim. 'Whether you believe it or not, Miss Knowles, the people who live under the shadow of Machapuchare *do*. Officials around here speak in hushed whispers of the beasts who will do Shiva's bidding should His sacred grounds be contaminated by the feet of man. The Destroyer will send forth his army to reap vengeance on the world.'

The chimes of pots and buoyant voices swamped the space left by Appleby's words. All of them were lost in the moment. Appleby broke their malaise.

'Now, I'm not saying that I believe in a great beastly army,' he said with a reassuring smile. 'But I do believe that there is something on that mountain, a creature of some sort, not mythical but something perhaps unexplained only because we haven't studied it yet.'

'I heard it was a bear,' Vine said. 'I watched something on National Geographic once.'

'I heard it was a monkey,' Hastings said.

'I heard it's all bullshit,' Knowles said. 'And this conversation ain't helping me change my mind.'

There was a pause before Appleby laughed. He pointed at Knowles and nodded enthusiastically.

'Science needs its sceptics, Miss Knowles,' he said wiping tears from his eyes. 'We must always begin any research study from an objective standpoint. Perhaps your best attribute on this expedition is to give us perspective from time to time.'

'This is a rescue mission though,' Hastings said. 'Not an expedition.'

'Of course,' Appleby said cautiously. 'Old habits die hard, as they say.'

***

At their hotel, Knowles sat on a small bench on the rooftop terrace, drinking coffee. Below her, the city Pokhara was swathed in a low mist, its convoluted buildings a mishmash of ancient history and red brick tenements. Flanking the city were hills made up of dense pine forests and open patches of grasslands the colour of rich emerald. The distant image of Machapuchare was an imposing backdrop even at this distance. Although she was a sceptic when it came to Appleby's worldview, she was in no doubt about how someone who believed in the mysteries of the world could be seduced by the mythos the great mountain evoked.

She drew in a breath and let go a sigh, savouring the silence about her. Knowles loved the early mornings. No matter where she was in the world, the thought of sitting watching the sun rise with her hands wrapped around a cup of good, strong black coffee always made her feel at peace.

Peace.

The word had always been a conundrum for her. In the days before her military career she had sought peace of a different kind;

respite from the emotional upheaval of a broken home and a life in turmoil. Her parents tried to do the right thing by her, tried to keep things amicable in her company. But for a fifteen year old girl, it seemed that parents had no understanding of how receptive affected kids were to the hushed war that raged behind living room doors. She found her peace at that time in Ronan Cullen, a kid who exuded attitude but always had time for her, and during these times always seemed to make her laugh with his buffoonery and shameless profanity. They had gone from friends to lovers in that uncertain time.

When the divorce was over, her father left to go back to distant family in Antigua, but her mother – a midwife – stayed at the family home and comforted her distraught daughter at the loss of her father. But emotions were raw, her mother became the object of contempt; the sense of abandonment fuelling the rage inside her. Knowles rebelled, staying out late, getting into trouble with the police for petty theft, and smoking blow. Ronan was forever her accomplice; they called themselves *The Joker* and *Harley Quinn*, and after they had committed a crime they would make love with their spoils about them.

This was to change the day she broke into the home of a local pensioner, Bertie Moyles. She'd had a row with Ronan, and he was talking about breaking up with her. Angry and disillusioned, she needed to let off steam. She went to the house with the intention of helping herself to any silverware she could pawn for booze and blow. But the homeowner had been sitting in his armchair as she came in through the window of the kitchenette.

He'd had thinning hair and walked with a cane, but always looked smart when out on the streets. This was why she had gone there. Someone who looked as dapper as Bertie Moyles was bound to have plenty to offer a petty thief.

She'd frozen when she saw him sitting in his armchair. He was staring right at her as she stood in the doorway separating the lounge from the kitchenette. It was several seconds before she realised that he was dead.

On his lap there was a photo album and it was open. Despite her fear and revulsion, she shuffled over to him and looked down at the photographs secured behind sheets of cellophane. They portrayed images of a life, Bertie's life, images of him as a young man, a teenager no older than she was at that moment; then there were wedding photographs and images of him in army uniform. He was sitting on a tank with several other men, all had their arms about each other; the sense of camaraderie clear to see.

One of his hands was on an image of his late wife, Elsie. Knowles knew she had died several weeks ago. Before her death, Bertie and Elise were inseparable. In the photograph Elise was in her wedding dress. Bertie's fingers were resting on the image and beneath them was a thin band of gold. A wedding ring - his *dead wife's* wedding ring.

Without thought, she had reached down and gingerly slid the ring from beneath the corpse's fingers. All the time her eyes flitted between her task and the dull glass of Bertie's eyes. She stepped away from him once she had the ring in her fingers. She held it up and scrutinised it. At that moment Knowles saw not the pawn shop and booze or blow. She saw just how low she was prepared to go in order to escape a life without peace. Emotion took her and she'd dropped the ring to the floor and hurried out of the house, back to her own bedroom where she had lain, guilt stricken and distraught, until her mother had returned home from her shift.

And she'd told her mother everything. But far from remonstrating and phoning the police, Mrs Knowles nodded and said she understood. From understanding came the foundations for change. Her mother had phoned the police to let them know that no one had seen Bertie, and they were worried for him; that he wasn't answering the front door. The police came to check, found him, and took it from there. But Knowles was to sit with her mother for most of the evening and go through what she needed to do to find the peace she was looking for and struggle with how she might be able to find it.

Then she remembered Bertie's photographs of him in the army; the images of him with his friends, big proud smiles on their faces, and that pervading sense of belonging to something bigger. It called to her, and she made the decision to join up within the same week. She told only her mother and by the end of that year was stationed in Afghanistan on her first tour.

From that point on, Knowles found that peace had many meanings. In joining the army she had sought out her emotional peace, but she became the tool of maintaining it on a far grander scale. The sense of purpose that came with such responsibility had never become lost on her. And now, as she stared out across the vibrant Nepalese city, sipping coffee and squashing the past, it had never been so clear.

Things weren't so clear cut at the moment though, were they? No, they sure-as-fuck-weren't. Despite the scenery, despite the escapade, this whole venture was leaving her unsettled; it was eroding her moment of reflection, nagging doubts surfacing like the screaming faces of demons from the netherworld.

She reached into her sarong and pulled free her phone. Then she called the man who, for many years, had been the vehicle for her ongoing sense of contentment.

***

'Hey,' Hastings said as he approached Knowles on the terrace. The sun was bright, and the distant flare from the snowy precipice of Machapuchare made him squint.

'Hey,' Knowles said.

'You said you wanted to talk,' he said when he got to her.

'Yeah.'

'So? We gonna do that or get breakfast?' he said.

'Something is fucking wrong here, Hastings,' she said. 'You have to see that, right?'

He shrugged his shoulders. 'What am I meant to see, Knowles?'

'This whole thing makes no sense,' she said.

'I ain't got nothing for you,' he said after a brief pause. 'It is as it is. A gig.'

'This is no gig like we've ever been on,' she said. 'This has got so many layers of bullshit you need a fucking tractor to get through it.'

'Then help me understand,' he replied.

She sat down on a low wall. Her sarong parted and revealed her taut thighs as she crossed her legs.

'Okay,' she said. 'I'll call it the way I fucking see it. This isn't a rescue mission. There isn't any Michael-fucking-Appleby stuck on that mountain.'

'And what makes you say that?'

'If I was rescuing someone and I had the cash Appleby has, I'd be on that mountain by now,' she said. 'No meals in restaurants, no overnight stays in fucking hotels.'

'You mean that's it?' he said sitting beside her. 'That's all you got?'

'I think it's enough to cast doubt on this whole thing,' she said.

'He has to coordinate this with the authorities on the ground, Knowles,' Hastings said gently. 'You know how getting the best Intel goes. These things take time.'

'So why does he need us?'

'Why do *you* think he needs us?' he countered.

'He let it slip last night,' she said with confidence. 'He called this *an expedition*. I think Appleby is going onto that mountain to find himself a fucking Yeti. And we're here to help him to do it.'

'So let's be clear,' he said. 'Appleby has brought an ex-black ops team to the Himalayas, not to navigate a covert way onto the mountain to find and rescue his lost son, but to help him bag a mythical ape-man?'

'You're putting it that way to make me sound fucking paranoid,' she said.

'Is that what you're saying or not?' he said. His tone was impatient, the sound of a man who has heard more than enough.

'Yes,' she said with defiance.

'So let's say you're right. What are we meant to do about that now?' he asked. 'We're stuck in the middle of a city with no ride home. And no current access to funds. Oh, and hang on, no fucking passports either. That's gonna take some explaining Appleby leaves us dumped here, and we need to head for the nearest international airport which I believe is over *five hundred kilometres from here.* If you got any ideas then how about you give them to me now?'

They glared at each other. But it was something neither could sustain for long. Hastings reached out and put a big hand on her shoulder. She allowed him to keep it there.

'Look. Knowles,' he said. 'I know this isn't our average gig. And yes, we don't know all the plays here. But for now we're stuck with it, okay? We'll get on the mountain. What's the worst that could happen if you're right? We brave the cold for a few days as this guy chases ghosts and snow leopard footprints. Or, if you're wrong and it really is a kosher gig, then we get him his son back. For sixty grand apiece, I call that a win/win.'

'Yeah,' she sighed. 'Okay.'

'Okay as in you're happy if we just go with it?'

'I'll be happy when I get a gun,' she said.

CHAPTER FIVE

After his discussion with Knowles, Hastings had made his way back to the hotel and found Grace in the lobby. He went over to her. As he stood by her side she was paying the bill with a platinum AA card. Her perfume smelled of cucumber.

'We good?' he said.

'Sure,' she replied as she pocketed her purse into a bright green cagoule. The material gave off a snake-hiss as she moved.

'Nice coat,' he said. It was meant to be cordial but felt clumsy.

'Need to blend in with the trekkers, right?' she replied with a flat tone.

'That's the plan,' he said.

Coming up with something from nothing was part of who Hastings was, what he had once excelled in when on the ground, odds stacked and bullets flying, calculating options with minimal Intel. Pity he wasn't as adept in his personal life. But as always when on a mission, he could compartmentalise, switching off any errant thoughts to focus on the plan.

And the plan was simple enough. Drive forty-two kilometres north to the town of Ghandruk. From there, the group would masquerade as tourists heading out to Annapurna base camp on foot, a walk of five hours where they would slip away and hit the southern approach to Machapuchare. Whilst the lower altitudes surrounding the mountain were sub-tropical which kept temperatures sitting around 14 degrees even in winter, the climate would change fiercely as they made their ascent. By the time they got to the coordinates spouted by Grace over dinner, temperatures could be as low as minus twenty degrees.

Appleby had been pre-emptive and made provision for this. Overnight he'd procured two blue Cherokee Jeeps - both battered with use in the harsh climate – and these were parked outside of the hotel amongst the bustle of passing cars and beaten up flatbeds. The jeeps were equipped with gear for an interim trip to the slopes. Tents and provisions were stored in ruck sacks which sat on hi-spec thermal clothing.

Hastings scanned the street, a habit of long standing when on a mission, his eyes flitting from one tenement to another, taking in the people milling around, those who were standing in small groups engaged in small talk. Across the street a heavy truck had its hood up, and a couple of burly looking truckers were pawing over the engine. One of them wore a bright red baseball cap that bobbed as his head dipped in and out of engine compartment. Hastings watched the hat for a few seconds before he was aware of Vine standing next to him.

'You keeping an eye out for ape men, chief?' Vine chuckled.

'Just keeping an eye out,' Hastings replied. 'Never hurts, does it?'

'That's a fact,' Vine said, heading for the Cherokee at the back of the two.

A few seconds later Hastings joined him.

***

Hastings and Johns opted for driving duties in their respective vehicles. Grace surprised them by getting in with Hastings' team, taking up position beside Knowles in the back seat, and leaving her father and Johns to travel together. The Cherokees stayed in close proximity, an easy feat given the heavy, slow moving traffic. At a crossroads on the outskirts of the city, Johns indicated right and merged into another run of vehicles making their way out into The Sanctuary as Hastings followed closely behind. From the back seat, Hastings looked at Knowles' face in the rear view mirror and smiled at the concentration he saw there, before something else caught his attention - a flicker of red - and noticed the truck that he'd seen outside the hotel was now a few cars behind them, the guy with the red baseball cap was riding in the passenger seat staring ahead.

'What is it?' Grace said.

'Nothing,' Hastings said. 'Just being paranoid.'

'Nothing wrong with that.' She laughed. It was a pleasant sound.

As they went north, the wide road that took them out of the city and into the foothills began to narrow and the terrain began to incline, the gradient subtle but enough for Johns and Hastings to put their respective vehicles in low gear.

'Fucking ears are popping like a bitch,' Knowles griped.

'Is it possible for you to say just one sentence without swearing?' Grace said.

'Fuck no,' Knowles said with a wink.

'She might not have charm,' Vine said, 'but she is predictable. If she ain't cursing, you got a good chance she's asleep.'

'Well, you haven't got any charm awake or asleep, arsehole,' Knowles said as she peered ahead. Beyond the glass, the branches of spruce trees wavered in the slipstream of the passing traffic. 'Never expected it to be like this out here.'

'I hear you,' Grace said. 'You say "Himalayas" to people, and most of them think of blizzards and ice. That's not to say they aren't a danger once we get on the mountain. But down here it has its own eco-climate. Gets as high as *twenty-six degrees* in the summer.'

'You know a lot about this stuff for a marine,' Hastings said.

'My *father* knows a lot about this stuff,' Grace replied. 'Which means I know a lot about it. But my brother is the real expert. He fell in love with this place when he was a child.'

'He came here as a kid?' Hastings asked.

'No. In his head,' she explained. 'In books. I guess he was drawn to the mystery of the place. The sense of adventure.'

'You mean the Yeti?' Vine said.

'Not at first,' Grace said after a pause. 'First of all, it was Mount Everest and Edmund Hillary's climb to the summit. Michael had such a fascination with our ability to overcome environmental adversity. He wanted to know how we came to be so risk aversive, and why people like Hillary challenged that belief. But when Hillary went on an expedition in the 1960s looking specifically for what was then known as *The Abominable Snowman,* Michael's interest was piqued.

She paused for a moment, her eyes distant. After a moment she returned back to them and continued. There was a grim smile on her lips.

'Yeah, Hillary came away from the mountains having analysed an alleged Yeti scalp that had been preserved in a monastery for over two hundred years and stories of large humanistic footprints. In the end, the scalp was said to be nothing more than the hide of an antelope goat, and the footprints were probably animal tracks that had been melted by the sun. Yet despite all of this, Hillary still believed in the possibility of the Yeti. And my brother and father hold a similar belief. Because Hillary still could not completely dismiss the idea as he could not *prove* that it *didn't* exist.'

'Shit, lady,' Knowles said as she shook her head. 'You even sound like your old man.'

'Comes from listening too much,' Grace said with a sigh. 'It's hard not to get swept away with it.'

'You saying you believe this Yeti business?' Hastings said.

'It doesn't matter what I believe,' she said, her tone firm. 'My family believes it, and we're on a mountain because of that belief. I do what I have to do.'

'I understand,' Hastings said.

'Fucked if I do,' Knowles said.

'Duty,' Hastings said. 'She's talking about duty.'

Grace's silence told them all that Hastings' assessment wasn't wrong.

***

Hastings snatched glimpses of Grace in the mirror. Her hair, pulled up into a bun on top of her head, let go small strands of gold that shimmied in time with the rocking cab.

She caught him looking, and a small smile played on her lips as he held her stare for as long as he dared before his eyes flicked back to the road ahead.

Stay focused, Hastings, his mind chided. *That woman is wrapped up like the prettiest gift in the world, but you don't know what's underneath the glitter.*

He had a good idea, though. There was no secret on what it took to become Special Forces, a level of determination and physical prowess that would leave the average man a gibbering wreck. Hastings was under no illusion: Grace Appleby was beautiful and deadly in equal measure.

He glanced up at the mirror again, intending to snatch one more intimate moment in her ice blue eyes. Instead, he saw the truck through the rear window; it was now directly behind them. It kept his eye; the red cap was close enough for him to see a white *Coke* logo splashed across the front of it.

'We got a tail,' he said.

'The truck?' Vine said, peering into his wing mirror.

'Saw it outside the hotel. It's been on our arse since Pokhara.'

'How can you be sure?' Grace said.

'That's what you're paying him for, honey,' Knowles said. 'If the man says it's a tail, it's a fucking tail.'

Grace pulled out her cell phone and hit the speed dial. Her father answered on the third ring.

'Someone's following us,' she said quickly. Appleby's voice fizzed in her ear.'Okay. Will let them know.'

'Know what?' Knowles said.

'We got problems up ahead, too,' Grace said.

'Like what?' Vine said. He leaned forward and peered through the windscreen as though this would somehow help Grace's comment gain more clarity.

'Seems a car's overturned. We got the start of a jam.'

'We got more than that,' Hastings said grimly.

'You thinking what I'm thinking, Chief?' Vine said.

'Ambush?'

'Seems like a hell of a coincidence, right?'

'Get your dad on the line,' Hastings said.

In the mirror Grace appeared puzzled but activated her phone.

'Put it on speaker,' Hastings said as Appleby answered. Grace did as he requested.

'Professor, listen up,' Hastings said. 'Tell Johns to follow my lead. You got that?'

'I'm not sure I …'

'Just do it, Professor,' Hastings said as he dropped the Cherokee into second gear. Appleby relayed the instructions to Johns.

Without warning Hastings yanked the wheel right and pulled out into the opposite lane. Grace and Knowles pitched left almost banging heads in the process. The phone tumbled from Grace's hands and landed in the foot well.

As he pulled out, Hastings was suddenly confronted by an oncoming grey Mazda. He swerved back in line as the car went by them, its horn screaming in time with the curses from the back seat.

'Jesus Christ,' Knowles hissed. 'See your driving is as shit as ever.'

The jeep powered back into the outside lane, Hastings thumping through the gears, climbing the road ahead which was currently clear.

He passed Johns' jeep as his eyes flitted to the rear view mirror. Sure enough, the truck that had been with them since the city pulled out and began its pursuit with a belch of grey-blue smoke.

Vine wound down his window and leaned out, trying to get a better look at their pursuers. The truck had a high windscreen so he was able to see the two large men sitting in the front seat. As well as the guy in the red cap, the driver was hunched behind the wheel, his face like stone, teeth gritted.

But it was his companion that had Vine's attention almost immediately. Because as well as his red *Coke* hat, the guy was crawling out of the passenger window and priming an AK47.

'Got an assault weapon incoming!' Vine said, ducking back inside the Cherokee. The next second the distant staccato pops of the AK47 came to them as the back windows shattered, and bullets chewed their way through the jeep.

Grace and Knowles hunkered down.

'Mother-fucker!' Knowles yelled. 'We need somethin' to retaliate with, Hastings!'

'We got nothing,' he said as another salvo came at them. They all hunched over, a bullet took out the windshield, and Hastings vision became a web of cracks. He felt the back of the jeep drop as tyres were shredded under the onslaught, and the terrible grinding sound came as the axle met the concrete road surface.

The wheel became unresponsive, and the vehicle skidded into an embankment where it came to a sudden stop. Small rocks and debris thudded against the bodywork like heavy rain. The occupants bounced around the cab as the chassis finally collapsed, but Hastings was booting open the door as soon as his head cleared.

He kept low, and watched as the truck came up the hill, the gunman still hanging out at of the window. As he took aim, Johns' jeep suddenly ploughed into the side of the cab. The gunman fought to keep hold of the weapon but Hastings watched as muzzle flashes flickered inside the cab of Johns' Cherokee.

The guy with the AK47 cried out as bullets caught him in the face and shoulder. The blood was a shocking crimson, making the baseball cap that flew off of his misshapen head suddenly pale in comparison. Gore splashed the driver who yelled in fury. From the dash he pulled a handgun and adjusted his position, pushing himself high in his seat so he could put three shots into the roof of Johns' jeep.

Johns swerved and ploughed into the truck with the awful sound of rending metal as the impact seemed to fuse both vehicles together for a brief moment.

The truck's tyre exploded as it ploughed into the embankment, and an explosion of rock and dirt reshaped the cab, frosting the windscreen as it gave way. As the truck succumbed to the onslaught, the momentum threw the driver forwards through the ruined windshield as a myriad of tiny glass cubes marked the moment for everyone looking on. The guy hit the road with a thud, and rolled violently across the concrete, limbs slapping against the hard surface, bones popping with a sickening frequency.

Johns pulled up beside the Hastings' jeep.

'Get in!' he yelled through the window.

'And go where?' Hastings said, looking up at the road ahead. A car was on its side, and the few people were standing beside it gawping at him. Oddly, some of them were in the police uniform, their red berets stark against the green foliage of spruce trees behind them, and no officer had made an attempt to respond to the events unfolding on the mountain. 'We're cut off.'

'Not for much longer,' Johns said. 'Now get the fuck in!'

'Language, Johns,' Knowles said as she jumped into the back of the jeep.

She was followed by the others who piled into the back seats. Hastings found Grace strewn across his lap. He looked down at her, their eyes locking for a few seconds.

'You got any other weapons?' Knowles said as Johns got the jeep moving again.

'Foot well,' Appleby whispered. He appeared distant with fear, his lips pressed together so tightly they were becoming white.

Grace adjusted herself in Hastings' lap, her firm buttocks and thighs briefly rubbing against his groin.

'What you doing, girl?' he muttered.

She sat upright and produced two Glock 19s. 'Merry Christmas,' she said flatly and handed the weapons to Knowles and Vine before stooping again to retrieve two more.

'You got anything else down there?' Hastings said as he took a Glock from her and actioned it.

'If this is pillow talk, it'll have to wait until later,' she said, and gave him a wink.

He shook his head in disbelief, but despite it all, a smile played briefly on his lips.

Ahead, the police officers who were supposedly tending to the accident ducked behind the overturned vehicle and began to unsling their weapons, standard SRLs of the Nepalese army. The five vehicles that had been stopped by the accident, a mishmash of cars and trucks, appeared ominously devoid of occupants.

'You happy now?' Hastings said as he watched Knowles prime her weapon.

'I'm getting there,' she said. 'Low risk, eh?'

Hastings shrugged his shoulders.

Knowles dropped her window and leaned out as the Cherokee steamed towards the road block. As the vehicle came within twenty yards of the accident site, rifle and small arms fire came at them from the police officers and several civilians.

Vine wriggled behind Knowles and shadowed her position through the window above her, their hands each holding their guns. Opposite them, Hastings and Grace replicated the manoeuvre.

'Open up,' Hastings said.

Four Glocks spat fire into the accident site. One police officer went down, his head an odd shape as a bullet worked it over. Another took a round to the shoulder. It spun him, and he disappeared behind the vehicle. There was a sense of hesitancy in those who remained. Rather than intensify their defences, they dropped out of sight.

'Get down,' Hastings said as he pulled himself back into the cab, Grace coming with him. 'They're going to spray the vehicle as we pass.'

'Only small arms fire left,' Knowles said. 'Who knows, we might just make it.'

Johns powered the jeep. They were still on the opposite side of the road so there was ample space for them to pass. But at the last moment, Johns swung the Cherokee so that it clipped the overturned vehicle, spinning it enough to have the would-be assailants emerging from cover in an attempt not to get crushed by the spinning bodywork.

Knowles came up and put bullets into two of them, scattering the others. The vehicle Johns had hit knocked two more into the bushes with short, sharp cries. By the time the ambush team had recovered, Johns had taken the jeep out of the range of their weapons.

***

'You want to tell me what the fuck that was all about?'

It wasn't Knowles spitting the profanities at Appleby. This time it was Hastings.

They had continued for several kilometres and pulled off the shrinking road into a thatch of forest ferns. The Cherokee reflected the state of its occupants: battered but still functional.

'This was meant to be low risk, Professor,' Hastings continued. 'Those were your words.'

'Can I ask you a question?' Appleby said softly.

'You going to answer mine?' Hastings said.

'Yes,' the professor said. 'I will, but let me first ask you this: what would you do to protect what you believe? Not the small stuff, but the things fundamental to *who you are*?'

'What the hell has that got to do with this?' Vine interjected, his voice was sharp and lacking patience.

'It means everything,' Hastings said. 'What just happened originates from the most basic of places.'

The puzzled expressions passed through *The Sebs* like a plague.

'Explain,' Hastings said. 'And fast.'

'The locals are afraid,' Appleby said. 'It is as I feared. This is a simple case of being protective of their superstitions and the possible repercussions should the un-natural order suddenly become unbalanced.'

'You fucking *expected* this?' Knowles spat.

'To a degree,' Appleby sighed. 'But I have to admit, I may have underestimated the response.'

'Are you shitting me?' Knowles began pacing. The undergrowth rustled beneath her agitated steps. 'Those fuckers were intent on killing us!'

'Why didn't you explain this as a possibility?' Hastings said. 'We could have prepared for it.'

'We have prepared for it,' Appleby said. He pawed thoughtfully at his beard. 'We brought weapons, for example.'

'That's as may be, but you were not transparent when you sold this to me,' Hastings said. 'And that kind of thing doesn't make me want to trust you.'

'I understand that,' Appleby said. 'But I guess you have to see this from my point of view. You had no real conviction in the reasons my son came here. No real belief in what may be with him on the mountain. Why would you understand the level of resistance in locals to us going up there? Would that have made the decision to come any different?'

Hastings appeared to consider this for a while. 'I know what men will do to protect their cause. So in that you have your answer. '

'I guess I do,' Appleby said.

'Don't explain how they were able to set us up,' Knowles said. 'Were those real police officers we shot?'

'More than likely,' Grace said. 'They'd be able to stage the accident site and prep it for us unchallenged.'

'Yeah,' Hastings said. 'And they could've arrested us and sent us packing at any point, too. This seems too …' 'He got stuck and paused.

'Radical?' Appleby offered. 'Yes. It is because these people have faith in the balance of things. They have belief and a deep rooted fear of what is in those mountains. And a need to make sure it never strays out of its lair. *The evil that men do* and all that, right?'

No one spoke for a few minutes as each mulled over recent events and the implications.

'So tell us, Professor,' Hastings said eventually. 'Tell us about this thing that has people so terrified they're prepared to murder their tourist trade.'

'Very well,' Appleby said. 'But first, I suggest we plan another route onto the mountain and get the devil out of here.'

No one argued with him.

CHAPTER FIVE

They dumped the Cherokee in the forest and dressed to ascend, their mountain gear light yet effective at sub-zero temperatures. They had lost two tents and some of their provisions when Hastings' jeep had crashed. Johns also informed them that a small weapons cache that had been stowed in a compartment in the boot had also been lost to them. This earned another prolific tirade from Knowles.

As it stood, they had handguns and four clips of ammunition each. Johns had produced a suppressed M4 from the boot of his own Cherokee.

'A regular fucking army,' Knowles said as she looked down at her Glock and the four clips. 'We run into a sustained firefight, and we're going to be pretty fucked.'

'Despite the probabilities of what we might run into, our main enemy for certain on the ascent is the cold,' Appleby warned. 'At this time of year, we get snow from the northeast; the wind chill will drop it down to minus twenty in exposed areas. '

'Right now the enemy is human and carries enough hardware to turn our vehicle into a colander,' Hastings said to Appleby. 'And I want to know who the fuck they are. *Now.*'

'They are *believers*,' Appleby said flatly.

'Meaning what?' Hastings replied with irritation in his voice. 'No more puzzles, Professor.'

Appleby sighed and nodded as if in resignation. He crossed his arms, the material of his cagoule hissing like an angry cobra.

'No matter what your personal position is with the existence of the Yeti,' he said to *The Sebs*, 'there is a group of people in Nepal who are devout to this beast. To them it is as real as you or me. They build their lives upon it; they exist only to serve its needs.'

'And what *are* its needs?' Vine asked.

'Well, if you ask those who choose to protect it, they would say it needs to be revered, like Shiva sitting at the summit of the mountain. And like most who have such a fundamental passion, their number will do anything to make sure its dominion remains sacrosanct.'

'Are you talking about some kind of fucking cult?' Knowles asked in disbelief.

'Their name translates as *The Order of the Mountain Man*,' Appleby said. 'But yes, they are devout and organised, a combination that does not make our job any easier.'

'And what about your son?' Hastings said. 'You say he may have fallen to the mountain. He could have easily have been ambushed by these fanatics.'

'The thought had crossed our mind,' Grace interjected. 'But the evidence wasn't there. You saw how these people work. They occupy prominent positions in the town, in local government. They don't want to be exposed any more than they need to be. Michael gave us no indication that he was followed onto the mountain.'

'But you can't be sure they weren't already waiting there for him,' Hastings assessed.

'That is true,' Appleby said.

'Or they aren't waiting for us,' Vine said.

'No,' Appleby conceded.

'You got any other surprises for us, Professor?' Hastings said. 'I can't plan anything in the dark. And I'm done second guessing the route.'

'Nothing more,' Appleby replied. 'Perhaps I should have been more open, but there was always the fear that you would not take the job, and we were pretty desperate to mount this rescue quickly.'

'Yeah,' Hastings said after acknowledging the professor's concession with a nod of his head. 'But we agreed to take on this mission, and if the same people who helped you find us told you how we work, then you should know we never renege on a deal. No matter how unstable the parameters may be.'

'I'm sorry,' Appleby said. His eyes met each of *The Sebs* in turn to reinforce his contrition. 'You now know as much as there is to tell.'

'Let's make this the last apology, Professor,' Hastings said. 'From this point on we got enough to be dealing with without having to worry about our client, too. We clear?'

'You have my word,' Appleby said. 'We are all on the same page here.'

'When it comes to chasing monsters, I very much doubt that,' Hastings said. 'But we got a common goal in finding your son. Let's just say that'll have to be enough.'

'We can find him with this,' Johns said, pulling a small black box from his coat. He hit a switch, and the slow bleep of a tracking device added to the sounds of the forest about them. 'Michael has a transponder with him.'

'Well, at least we're not totally in the dark,' Vine said.

Hastings turned away from the professor and addressed Grace.

'You got a map?' he asked.

Grace pulled out a small folded tourist map and handed it to Hastings. He unfolded it, went down to his haunches, and laid it on the ground. His finger followed an imaginary trail on the smooth paper.

'Let's see if we can find a way onto the mountain without getting killed before we get there,' he said to the others.

'As a plan, that works for me,' Vine said.

***

They hit the east slope of Machapuchare after three hours of steady walking. Hastings' route added another two kilometres to their journey as they circumvented the town of Ghangruk for fear of ambush. They stopped once to take in a little water and energy bars, the mood sombre as the brooding, majestic shape of the mountain loomed ahead. To the northwest was the Annapurna base camps; four purpose-built villages made up of several oblong prefabricated structures. In the summer season, there would be an overspill of tents strewn across the plateau, but at that moment the hikers at the base camps were few, and only scattered tents were pitched here and there, the wind from northwest rustling the weatherproofing with thick oscillating sounds that came to them across the valley.

Diamox pills kept their metabolisms in check, fending off altitude sickness, and the steady incline took them to over four thousand metres as they began their ascent. Johns kept hold of the location device, and its steady beep guided their way through the surrounding terrain.

On the slopes, Vine took point, Johns giving him the M4 as company, an agreement they had made prior to the ascent. Vine peered at the terrain ahead, his snow goggles keeping the chill breeze from bringing tears to his eyes, yet giving the whole landscape a sickly yellow tint. The ground was a mix of uneven rock dusted with snow, and course grass that pierced the frosting. He placed his feet carefully, navigating the road ahead with total and utter caution.

Acute awareness, mental dexterity in the proximity of potential danger, was the skill needed on point, honed over several tours with 42nd Commando. But, before the army, caution and commitment had never always been bedfellows in Patrick Vine's life. In fact, they were attributes that were so distant from his current mind-set they sometimes felt as though they had been stolen from someone else. Vine was okay with this; he was a very different person to the man who had taken the Queen's Shilling.

Vines' father and grandfather had both served, each of them carving careers that had built the foundations of family tradition. His father - a big man with a disciplinarian approach to parenting - had eventually served as a sergeant in the Military Police. Vine's mother was a timid yet impatient woman who dulled the instability of her husband's postings with Gordon's Gin. She had died of liver cirrhosis when Vine was sixteen and his father was based at Norton Barracks in Worcestershire. The close knit community of service wives supported Patrick through the grieving process, each with a gentle well-meaning platitude, imparted with slurred speech. He had lost a mother; they'd lost a drinking sister.

Those were heady days indeed, and Vine managed to avoid the trap of using gin and cold comfort to cope with his loss.

Instead, he'd chosen to get the hell away from everything associated with life before his mother's death. He left his father a note. In it he explained that, although there was always an unsaid expectation that he too would follow suit and join up, he had no intention of doing so; he never wanted the same dispossessed lifestyle for his future family.

Even now his naive edict all those years ago made Vine smile behind his face scarf. As a seventeen-year-old running away from a past, Vine found out pretty quickly it wasn't a case of logistics. Yeah, he got a job stocking shelves in a supermarket chain; yeah, he made enough to cover rent for a crummy bedsit in Dudley. But he couldn't escape his upbringing; the kind of stuff ingrained in his personality. He was self-sufficient and self-reliant, tenets inherited from his background, but this did not come without recourse. He was slave to a failure to be able to commit to anything - or anyone - for that matter. Relationships were a mere facade, one night stands or awkward mistakes he left to drift until women made the decision to end it. His apathy was the only constant; his life devoid of the emotional meaning to give him the glue to help connect and commit to relationships. On the day he decided to go back to his father, one of these relationships was coming to an end.

Kath Foster was a colleague from work. She was a single mother, and Daisy, her daughter, was three years old. Vine had met Daisy only once in the eight weeks the relationship had lasted, the day before Kath had called it all off, in fact. It had come as a surprise to Vine, yet Kath was keen to find someone to be a father for Daisy, offering a level of stability that Vine himself had craved. For a moment, this thought had struck him when Kath had cited his hesitancy around Daisy as her reason for ending it. She simply could not take the risk of having her daughter being emotionally hurt again if Vine decided to leave. He understood, and told her as much. The irony was, for the first time, he actually felt something when Kath walked away, a small ache in his heart that gave him enough insight to know he could run from his past, but it would always cling to him, steering him in directions of its choosing, ultimately guiding him back to his roots - back home -

where father was waiting with a grim, knowing smile, and a draft card.

Over several beers, father and son spoke their piece, the alcohol giving Vine a nudge, but his taste of life away giving him the greatest courage to speak his mind. His father merely nodded, and eventually told his son that he could find belonging and purpose by signing on the line. And such was the conviction in his father's voice, and such was the need for connection with something that made him no longer feel meaningless, he scrawled his signature on the papers shortly before this father reached across and shook his son's hand.

'One day all will be clear to you, Patrick,' he'd said.

From that point, he experienced what it felt like to belong, consistency found in the squad, the platoon, the company, the band of brothers and sisters, his father's words finally making sense.

On the slopes of Annapurna, Vine allowed the chill wind to sweep these memories away. The breeze brought something else with it: nebulous clouds turned yellow by his goggles.

Vine stopped and turned to the others who were also staring at the sky.

'Storm front!' Appleby yelled to them all. 'We need to set up shelter or we'll be caught in a whiteout!'

'How long we got?' Knowles said, watching the burgeoning clouds rolling in at an alarming rate. Hastings was stood at her shoulder.

'Well know soon enough,' he said grimly. 'Let's get to it.'

They moved closer to the mountain and found an expanse of grassland juxtaposed by a sheer wall of jagged rock. Here they quickly set up their camp - three tents, one to house their gear, the others for the storm-battered group - were secured to the ground by hi-visibility guy ropes made of lime green nylon, and heavy duty cleats were hammered into the firm surface with a large rubber mallet that Johns wielded like a pro.

Within twenty minutes of making their appearance, the great clouds blotted out the sky, and the mountain succumbed to a grim twilight. A fierce, steady stream of icy wind washed over the three tents, their material sagging in places under the onslaught. The snow was smog thick, a swirling white maelstrom that brought visibility to mere feet. The cold had come with it. Johns had planted a thermometer outside the tent he was sharing with Appleby and Grace, and the device told them the outside temperature was reading minus fifteen.

The Sebs hunkered down inside their own tent, faces starkly illuminated by a solar powered lamp, listening to the howling wind and the driven snow scratching against the canvas walls like thousands of tiny claws.

The storm hit them hard for over six hours, keeping them in their tents, secured against the biting cold by layers of Thinsulate, and heavy quilted sleeping bags. They communicated with Appleby through walkie-talkies until there was an acceptance that they would need to stay put and see the storm through.

As night fell, the camp bedded down, Hastings keeping first watch, mind steeled, ears listening out for anything beyond the storm. He was two hours into his shift when he heard the sound of heavy movement outside the tent.

***

Hastings fought against the waves of tiredness by thinking of his daughter. It was a trick he'd used many times when in the field. The image that he held onto was the day he first saw Poppy. She had been two months old, and he'd missed her birth while on a deep recon in Syria.

Poppy had been in her cot at the family home in Wythall, Worcestershire, and the overwhelming sense of love and joy at the tiny, sleeping infant swathed in an oversized pink baby grow had left him breathless. It was a memory that he could summon at will, and he was relishing the moment when the sound of crunching snow came to him.

The wind had died down to intermittent gusts, and at first Hastings thought the strange environment was playing tricks on him. He subconsciously leaned forward in order to make some kind of distinction between facts or the trickery hyper vigilance sometimes played on the senses of those on sentry duty.

Hastings went through the probabilities as he unzipped his sleeping bag and primed his weapon. It could be someone from the other tent risking a quick piss in the subdued storm. Or it could be *the believers* who tried to ambush them on the road.

The footfalls came again, heavy and lumbering.

Closer.

He could also hear something else. Ragged, rhythmic sounds.

Breathing.

For the first time in as long as he could recall, Hastings froze. Something wasn't right, and that something suddenly let go a low reverberating growl that seemed to oscillate every bone in his body.

He nudged his crew who woke grumbling, but he cut them short with a finger to his lips. He signalled there was a problem by pointing at the canvas walls with pistol shaped fingers. Knowles and Vine slowly extricated from their sleeping bags and readied their weapons.

The growl came again, stuttering this time as something dragged in a breath.

Knowles appeared wide eyed and brought up her Glock.

Hastings waved an open hand, his palm down, and his message clear. *Take it easy. We got to figure out what the hell is going on.*

But no sooner had Hastings done this, a short sharp cry of fear came to them through the canvas.

The gunshots came a split second later.

CHAPTER SIX

The Sebs emerged from their tent as efficiently as the cramped space and heaped snow would allow. The storm had bleached the landscape, and although the rock walls had protected their camp to some extent, there were three foot drifts in the doorway that they had to plough through before they could stand upright.

The blizzard had moved on and day break was rolling in from the east, a brilliant red ribbon marking out the horizon. Hastings and the others brought up their guns and tracked the scene as they sought out a target.

'Look over there,' Vine hissed as he aimed his M4 at a landmark ahead. Twenty metres away, in the murky light, a patch of ground had been churned up in the pristine landscape about their camp. There were twin trails in the deep snow that marked the passing of someone or *something*. Hastings followed the trail back and noted that it lead from Appleby's tent just as the professor and Grace began emerging from their tent, faces stark against the blue material, but the concern was also there.

Grace had her pistol raised.

The Sebs lowered their weapons as Grace ploughed over to them.

'Johns is missing,' she said with concern.

'He got off a few shots,' Hastings said.

'Yeah, we heard,' she said sharply. 'Because we aren't deaf.'

'Looks like there was a struggle over there,' Hastings said cutting her some slack. Johns was her comrade after all.

They all faced the patch of disturbed snow.

'What was he struggling with?' Knowles said. She sounded confused.

'Cover me,' Hastings said as he headed out.

'I'm coming with you,' Grace said. Her face was rigid, her eyes like steel.

Hastings shrugged, and they both made their way through snow that came up to their knees. As they neared the site of the disturbance, they stopped as though some invisible barrier had barred their way.

The snow was strewn about, but this was only part of the story. Beyond the site was a series of huge indents, tracks of some sort, leading to and from their camp. What was of particular concern, was that such tracks were too big to be that of a man, even with Johns' stature. And what was more, they only made the shapes of footprints, almost as if whatever had made them was light enough to walk over the surface of the landscape as though the snow was mere inches deep.

'Look at this,' Hastings said to Grace as he inspected the churned snow. Grace looked down at his gloved finger as he pointed to the ground where a crimson spot, no bigger than a penny, lay crystallised on the ice.

Blood.

***

There were three further blood spots a few feet away. They lay at intervals amongst the line of footprints heading off, away from their camp, before veering right and ascending the rocky slope. The trail disappeared behind a huge rock that looked like the decaying canine of a huge, ferocious beast.

They were all standing around the site where the snow had been disturbed. The blood spot was now a scarlet stain in the snow as the sun cast its light across the mountain. Overhead the sky was cobalt with high clouds; a stark contrast to the previous day.

'Only one set of tracks leading away from camp,' Vine noted.

'Must've carried Johns with it,' Hastings said. 'Minimal blood loss. He may still be alive.'

'Maybe he bagged an animal and went after it,' Knowles said.

'Johns wouldn't do anything as reckless as leaving camp without informing us,' Appleby said. He appeared concerned; his eyes kept flitting to the tracks leading away from them. 'And what do you mean by "it"?'

'I heard something before the gunshot,' Hastings said. 'Something was growling. Something big.'

'You mean like a snow leopard?' Knowles said. She sounded hopeful.

'A snow leopard would make more of a mess than this,' Vine said. 'Those things go for the throat. Plus, Johns' weapon has gone.'

'Vine's right,' Appleby said to Hastings. 'But you know that already, don't you?'

'I don't know *what* I know, Professor,' Hastings said as he looked at the footprints snaking away across the mountain. 'Maybe one of those weirdoes from the ambush snuck up here and took him. Maybe they had snow shoes. Fact is your man is gone, and he's more than likely alive, for now at least. Question is what we gonna do about it?'

'The question is *what the fuck took him*,' Knowles interjected. 'Those aren't snowshoe prints, Hastings, and you know it.'

Appleby appeared perplexed. For the first time on their mission the professor seemed indecisive. He stood looking down the mountain and then back to the camp as though trying to find answers anywhere he could.

'So, what are we going to do, Professor?' Hastings said.

'We have to find Johns,' Appleby said eventually.

'You mean go and find whatever took him,' Vine said with a scowl. 'You think it's a Yeti, right?'

'There is no denying my curiosity – or my excitement – for that matter,' Appleby said, though did not appear to be showing either of those emotions when he spoke. 'My interest is purely pragmatic. Johns has the tracking device on him. It's the only way we can find my son.'

They all stood in silence, and a gust of icy wind took their breath away for a few seconds.

'Then we have no choice at all,' Hastings said. He turned to his team. 'Break camp. Knowles, you're with me. Vine, you're to protect our client. We clear?'

'You got it, Chief,' Vine said. He didn't look too happy about his assigned duties, but Hastings continued regardless,

'We good with this?' he said to Appleby and Grace.

'Yes,' Appleby said, his teeth juddering under the cold.

'Get inside,' Hastings said. 'We'll stay in touch via radio.'
Without another word, everyone went about their duties.

***

Before leaving the camp, Hastings swapped his Glock for
Vine's M4. Knowles took two extra clips for her Glock from
Grace. They had gone about the exchange in silence. They were
no goodbyes or well wishes. This was just another job; a mission
like countless others executed in the line of duty.

Hastings clipped the walkie-talkie to his webbing, and the
low static hiss kept them company as both he and Knowles waded
through snow that was, in parts, thigh-deep.

The tracks lead them around a cliff face. Beyond this a huge
horseshoe-shaped inlet had shielded the rocks from the blizzard,
creating a basin of snow only as deep as their boots. On the
threshold of this basin, they both caught their breath.

Knowles scanned the locale as she took air only partially
warmed by her face scarf. She saw something fifteen feet above
them - an entrance barely visible amongst the mountain's ragged,
undulating exterior.

'Cave!' she said, pointing with her Glock. Sure enough, a dark
rough archway was embedded in the rock. It was served by a
ledge that jutted out like the lip of a sulking toddler. Knowles
understood that she'd been lucky to spot the cave. Had the tracks
not led them to a dead end, she would not have spotted it.

Hastings' eyes followed the ledge and saw a series of indents
in the cliff face. They were sequential - made rather than evolved-
each one higher than the next.

'Access?' he said nodding towards the in-cuts.

Knowles shrugged, and they went over for closer inspection.
As they neared they saw the small square nodules of rock either
side of holes clearly hewn into the rocks.

'Shit, Chief,' Knowles whispered. 'Someone made these. We
don't know what the fuck it is.'

Hastings looked at her through his yellowed goggles.

'Stay on mission, Knowles,' he said. 'It's the enemy. That's all we need to remember. You want help with perspective then look at your feet.'

Knowles did so and saw more blood spots in the snow. She nodded.

'We climb up,' he said. 'We shoot anything that isn't Johns. We clear?'

'Got it.'

Hastings shouldered his weapon and reached up for the squared hand holds. He placed a boot into the indent. Slowly and assuredly, he began his climb into the unknown.

***

Deep within the cave an inert shape lay in a heap, limbs twitching, the movements producing small groans of discomfort.

After a few moments, Johns rolled onto his side. He coughed and spat phlegm. Carefully he pushed himself upright, wincing at the movement, his mind adjusting as consciousness returned.

The first thing that came to Johns was the smell. It was a cloying mix of sweat and cheese, making him gag. He brought a hand up to his mouth; wiped it. His cheek smarted, and he sucked in air until the pain subsided. Gingerly he touched his incisors. They were both loose.

'Fuck.'

The word was thick, and came from lips that felt twice the size. He looked about him; the sparse surroundings were lit by a murky half-light, a large chamber with jagged, undulating walls of rock, stalagmites and stalactites like teeth, and within the wall, veins of bright silver that gave off a twinkling illuminance, filling the chamber with its grey, cream light.

As his vision acclimatised to this eerie netherworld, so it was he tried to recall what had happened; how the hell he'd ended up in this place. Images came to him - flicker flashes - like monochrome frames of silent movies he used to watch with his ailing grandfather on the Birmingham housing estate where he'd grown up; before the days of videos, DVDs and digital downloads. Before the army and the time spent afterwards where his services, like so many like him, were sought by those prepared to pay.

He recalled needing a piss, he recalled moving far away enough from the camp to take it in privacy. Then he remembered something lumbering out of the gloom, a huge shape, standing upright like a man. He'd pulled his Glock, taking aim and could've sworn he'd fired into the mass of fur at point blank range. His vision had been obscured by a huge hand, and then the lights went out.

Now he was here. Wherever the hell "here" was. Johns scanned the cave floor in the fragile hope the Glock was somewhere nearby. He laughed to himself when the search proved to be as futile as he thought it would be.

Placing a steadying hand on the nearby wall, he made to stand. He was surprised to find that warmth seeped through his gloved palm as through the silvery lines in the rock were giving off heat as well as light. But he also felt something else - pulsating vibrations like the heart of a great beast. Johns pushed away ridiculous childhood notions of fire breathing dragons swooping from the sky and laying villages to waste with great gouts of searing flame.

He stood, taking a few seconds to make sure he still had his balance. His vision blurred momentarily, making him swallow hard, and blink rapidly. There was a disturbing heat in his belly, a sensation he'd never experienced before. He removed his hand from the wall, and it took him a few seconds to realise that the pulse he'd felt in his palm was now replicated as a low, oscillating whine in his ears. He took several cautious steps; painfully aware the thing that had brought him here could appear at any moment. If he needed any form of motivation, it was in the thought of that hulking mass of fur stepping into the chamber.

As unsteady as he was, Johns went in search of escape.

*****

Vine checked over his handgun.

'You checked that twice already,' Grace said.

'And I'll check it again if I want to,' he said bluntly. 'We got caught out twice now. It's not happening a third time.'

Grace looked at him; her eyes were narrowed with disapproval.

They were inside Appleby's tent. Vine had tried to remain outside, but the biting wind had driven them all back under cover.

'It's bad enough I got stuck babysitting you two,' Vine griped.

'There's only one child in this tent,' Appleby said pointedly. 'Perhaps it would be better for all if you kept your reservations to yourself.'

'I can do that,' Vine growled. 'Don't make it any less true.'

'What is truth, Vine?' Appleby said. 'A set of events that everyone will see differently or interpret in a way that suits their own ends.'

'Maybe,' Vine admitted. 'But given that you're the guy who wants the existence of these things to be real, you don't seem too impressed by it.'

'It is a bitter sweet day,' Appleby said. 'The existence of the Yeti is a step closer to becoming a reality. But it also means what has happened to my son becomes even more perilous.'

At this Grace tried to suppress a moan, but her voice betrayed her.

'I need some air,' she managed.

There were tears in her eyes, and she moved past Vine towards the exit.

'We need to stay together,' Vine called after her, but Grace shut off his words by zipping the tent flap closed. The sound of her boots crunching through the snow crust began to fade as she put distance between her and the camp.

'You certainly have a way with people,' Appleby sniffed.

'Well, you ain't paying me to be a counsellor,' Vine sulked. After a few moments, he made for the exit.

'Better go and check on her,' he said. 'You coming?'

Appleby nodded. He fished around the tent for his goggles. 'I'll follow you out.'

Vine unzipped the exit and clambered outside. He strapped on his goggles and face scarf, looking momentarily to the east where

Hastings and Knowles had headed off after Johns, to face God knew what.

He wanted to believe their foe was human; something that would succumb to either gun or reason. Yet as fantastic as the premise was, the realities of war made it clear to Vine that human adversaries were not responsible for Johns' abduction. Humans would have had difficulty overpowering someone like Johns; the guy was a powerhouse, and humans would also have taken out the entire camp. Even now his mind was so tuned into the *Art of War* it continued to seek a military explanation for what was going on. Perhaps there was a black ops team on mission, but again he knew the tactics on show were not part of any covert parameters he was aware of, no matter how much he searched his mind.

He sucked frigid air through his face scarf as he spotted Grace two hundred meters away from their camp, her lime green coat shocking against the blanched landscape. She was standing with her back to him, and he made to walk forwards when a sound caught his attention. It was a sequence of high pitched, electronic beeps that emanated from Appleby's tent. The sound made Vine curious. It made him pause and slowly turn, his movements measured; training and instinct fusing seamlessly. Another gust of freezing wind tousled the snow, and Vine used it to move to the tent and crouch outside the opening. The bleeps continued but their volume was muted. Now nearer to the tent, Vine recognised the sounds and became confused because the device that was making them was not meant to be inside the tent at all.

With the growing breeze as his cover, Vine drew up the zip and peered inside the tent. Appleby looked up, so startled by Vine's presence that he almost dropped the location device in his hand. Instead he managed to grasp it and stow the black box swiftly in the pocket of his Cagoule.

'What you got there, Professor?' Vine said firmly.

The look on Appleby's face was that of a contemptuous schoolboy who had been caught lying to his teacher.

'This has nothing to do with you, Vine.' The professor's tone was harsh and matched the cold fury in his eyes.

'That looked like the GPS tracker,' Vine said, helping the professor out. 'I thought Johns had it on him when he was taken? In fact, I specifically remember you telling us, and that's why Hastings and Knowles are risking their arses on a search and rescue mission to bring that motherfucker back here.'

Appleby's response surprised Vine. The professor's demeanour changed from petulant child to that of a man who was in control, *in command,* his mouth turning into a smile and his shoulders relaxed.

'This is bigger than Johns,' he said. 'It's bigger than you and the rest of your team.'

'Yeah,' Vine said. 'I get it, a potential *'find of the century'*; fame and an even bigger fortune than you have already.'

Appleby surprised him again by laughing. 'What we have found here isn't a boon, you idiot,' he spat. 'It is intriguing I'll grant you that, but to be frank, it is an irksome distraction to what is in play.'

'And what is in play here, Professor?' Vine said.

'That would be telling,' Appleby whispered.

There were two small, fat sounds, and Vine's eyes saw a bizarre sight as the hip pocket of Appleby's cagoule seemed to erupt in two places. Then his world was consumed by pain as low calibre bullets punched into his upper chest and face. His lower jaw fractured with a crack, the emerging cry of pain drowned out by blood and teeth as they sought out his gullet.

Vine staggered backwards and collapsed outside in the snow, the blood steaming momentarily in the heat before being whipped away by the wind. Where it seeped onto the ground, it began to freeze, becoming nothing but crimson slush as it pooled around Vine's head.

Appleby stood over him, the suppressed Glock now exposed to the ambushed man, and his face was a mask of cold contempt.

'You had to snoop,' Appleby said to the dying man. 'You had to try and be more than you are: *a grunt,* an employee.'

Vine's chest pumped up and down as he tried to get oxygen to lungs slowly filling with blood.

'Well, I guess I'm going to have to terminate your contract,' Appleby said.

If Appleby had decided on the severance package, it was the Glock that signed the paperwork.

***

'What the fuck have you done?' Grace said with exasperation.

Both she and Appleby were standing over Vine's body.

'This one was becoming a fly in the ointment, dear Grace,' Appleby said casually. 'I am to blame in some respects. My concern with finding what is ours is making me a little impatient.'

'This changes things,' she said. She shuffled on the spot as though uneasiness was getting the better of her. Appleby put and arm about her waist, and she rested her head on his shoulder.

'No, it doesn't,' he said.

She turned to face him, and there, with Vine's body still cooling in the Nepalese air, the two of them kissed deeply. After a few moments, they parted and turned back to Vine.

'What about Johns?' she said.

'We knew the potential for casualties,' he said. 'He knew that as well as any of us.'

'But not like this,' she said. '*The Sebs* are meant to mitigate any risk to us.'

'And under normal circumstances, that would have been the case, my love,' he said. 'But we have to accept that we are not alone on this mountain. Something is muddying the waters, be it man or beast. We need Hastings and Knowles to complete what we have started.'

'So how do we explain this?' she said.

'We have a monster on the loose do we not?' Appleby said staring down at Vine. 'Get the ice pick from the tent.'

***

Knowles and Hastings edged their way through the cave. Once they had climbed to the entrance, they had radioed Appleby to update him. The professor had responded after a few calls, and acknowledged their update in an even and sedate tone.

The entrance gave way to a meandering tunnel that went a quarter of a mile before opening out into an ante-chamber. They had started out using their torches, but the initial darkness had given way to a murky twilight as they moved through the subterranean world.

'Look at this,' Hastings said,, pointing at the silver streaks appearing in the rocks.

He reached up and stroked a vein, bringing his hand away to inspect his fingertips.

'Warm to touch,' he observed. 'What the hell is it?'

'Fucking strange is what it is,' Knowles said.

'Let's just get this thing done, okay?' Hastings whispered.

'Whatever "this thing" is,' she muttered. 'I'm not hopeful of Johns' current condition being anything other than *fucked up*.'

'You may well be right. But we still need the tracking device to complete our objective,' Hastings reminded her.

'Operational parameters are unstable as fuck,' she replied. 'What happens if we don't find him?'

'We review options,' he said. 'Now, enough chatter. Let's stay focused.'

They continued for several hundred metres, the environment unchanging, a bleak and featureless series of tunnels and chambers. Beneath their feet, the ground continued on an incline, the air becoming stale and infused with an unsettling smell of rotten meat. At the far end of another chamber, Hastings pulled them to a halt.

'What is it?' Knowles said.

'Look ahead,' he said as he pulled his torch from his webbing. As he activated it, the concentrated beam washed a section of rock, revealing something etched onto the undulating surface: a cave painting depicting several crude figures. They appeared as men, but there were roughly drawn vertical lines from each limb, and their foreheads and jaws jutted forwards, making their heads appear concave.

Each figure was either carrying a misshapen club or spear; those that did not had thrown these makeshift weapons into the air where a cylindrical shape with oversized beak and small wings hovered between two inverted 'V' shapes.

'How old you do think this is?' Knowles said with fascination.

'Appleby might be a better person to ask,' Hastings said. 'He might be able to interpret what it means too. It might be useful Intel on the enemy.'

'Maybe we could radio it in?' Knowles said. 'Get him here?'

'We need to stick to our objective,' Hastings said. 'Johns is counting on us to be responsive; the mission is, too.' He turned off his torch.' This is for another time.'

It was as they prepared to move into the next chamber that three huge shapes rose from the shadows of nearby rocks, each one bringing with it the stink of spoiled meat, and a deep rumbling growl.

CHAPTER SEVEN

As Johns made his way through the seemingly endless tunnels and chambers, he fought off waves of panic each time he thought of being trapped underground forever. His military training helped to some degree, yet childhood fears were never far away, keen to erode his resolve, and sending him into seconds of panic that left him breathless.

Kenneth, his older brother, had a mean streak. Part of exercising that involved teasing his younger brother throughout their childhood. But Ken's masterpiece of childhood bullying came on the day he tricked a ten-year-old Johns into believing that their Christmas presents had been hidden in the basement of their family home. While their parents were out running errands, Ken had lured Johns into the basement. And then locked him in.

For six hours.

Despite the pounding on the door, the curses, and the pleading, Ken kept the door locked. At first came the laughter and the taunts, but then came the bad stuff: stories of things roaming around in dark cellars, things with claws and teeth, and a taste for young children.

He'd only let Johns out when he knew their parents were due back home. And then he'd denied it all, saying that Johns was trying to get him into trouble for no reason at all.

Whether his parents believed Ken or not was an irrelevance to the traumatised Johns. He avoided dark places for years as a result and refused to stay at home alone with his brother ever again.

It was the army that helped him to address his fears. Intensive night training had a habit of rooting out phobias and beating them to death. It was either that or failure, and Johns didn't like failing any more than he used to hate the dark. Failing made him feel weak; it took him back to the times he was subservient to his hateful brother. Yeah, his brother finally got his when his nefarious antics followed him into adulthood and put him in jail for life after he killed someone for their Rolex. But Johns could not glean any kind of satisfaction from his brother's self-destruction as he'd personally had no hand in it.

Now these things were mere memories, almost like some distant nightmare, but the darkness and its emotional residue was very real. The ever-present heat in his stomach didn't help either. It felt strange, an alien sensation that made him think of terrible diseases and infections that could be eating away at his insides.

Johns paused to stave off another wave of anxiety, his breathing deep and controlled, techniques taught by his SAS instructors at Hereford. He paused and used the time to curse his brother under his breath.

When he heard the heavy footsteps and ragged breathing nearby, he held onto the oxygen until his lungs became curtains of steel in his chest. The strange sounds came from a nearby entrance to what he could low see as another chamber. This was different in that the silvery light seemed brighter inside it, and long undulating shadows are moving along the floor.

Moving towards him!

Johns dropped down as two shapes emerged, and he exhaled despite his awe at the sight now before him.

They were humanoid and covered in brown fur. Even hunched at the shoulders they were big; Johns estimated at least seven feet tall, their broad bulk giving them even greater stature. Their foreheads were high and pushed forward slightly; the lips of their ape-like muzzles were made uneven by large, malformed teeth.

Despite the circumstances, despite witnessing the potency of these incredible creatures first hand, Johns shook his head in wonder. Myth had become reality.

As had the danger.

Yet the motives of these beasts remained uncertain. They had snatched him from camp as though he was nothing more than a child's toy; they could've killed him, torn him to pieces with their bare, massive hands. To understand this enemy, the soldier in him needed intel. Then he needed to get the hell out of there and get back to the real mission.

The humming sound in his head continued to oscillate. As the creatures moved towards him, he hunkered down behind a large rock, the hum appearing to intensify to a level where his eye sockets vibrated, sending dizzying waves of pain behind his eyes, the pressure making him groan with pain. His mouth filled with acidic bile as the heat in his belly radiated up his throat. He crumpled to his knees, his hands going to his temples, palms clamped to the side of his head as though trying to squeeze the badness out of his brain.

The sounds of hurried feet came to him accompanied by the snarls of nearby creatures. He felt hands on his body and waited for them to rip him to pieces.

Then suppressed gunfire sent fat hissing sounds around him, the din sending dagger blades of pain through his skull causing him to cry out. A small urgent voice cut through his agony as hands began to drag him to his feet.

'Get on your fuckin' feet, moron,' Knowles said. 'I'm rescuing your sorry arse.'

***

Knowles and Hastings brought up their weapons simultaneously; the three creatures before them came snarling and slapping the walls in fury but were keeping their distance.

'Why aren't they charging at us?' Knowles said.

'It's a display,' Hastings said as he watched the Yeti posture and peel their lips wide in order to bare their teeth. He's seen this before on David Attenborough's *Life on Earth* re-runs. 'A show of strength. But we've got to get past 'em. They're between us and the next chamber.'

'Our options are limited,' Knowles said. 'Maybe we could neutralise the threat or one of us leads them away.'

'This is their turf,' Hastings said. 'We're at a disadvantage. We have to take them down.'

Knowles was hesitant.

'What is it?' Hastings asked.

'Seems wrong killing them,' she said as she took aim. 'We only just discovered 'em.'

'Yeah,' he said. 'But the mission is all, Knowles. You know it.'

'Sure,' she said. 'Maybe we take out the one in the middle and the others might scatter?'

Hastings raised the M4 and dotted the largest Yeti. The red spot barely wavered on the beast's huge chest.

'It's all or nothing,' Hastings said. 'Can't have them regrouping if there are more of them.'

Knowles acquiesced with a nod.

'Put them down!' Hastings yelled.

The carbine spat rounds into the Yeti in Hastings' scope. The beast took several steps backwards as the salvo punched ragged holes into its chest, and to Hastings' surprise yellow, viscous fluid pumped from the wounds. Incredibly, the creature gave out a furious snarl and powered forward again, a charge driven by savage retribution. Hastings put a bullet into its eye, slapping the head to the left with such force a terrible crack could be heard as the neck fractured. The beast seemed to stagger around blindly before smashing into a nearby wall, and then toppled over, hitting the floor with a thump. Grey dust rose like a ghostly smog. The Yeti's companions appeared frozen by the assault, their hesitancy giving Knowles time to follow Hastings' lead and take one of them down with two rounds to the head. Undeterred by the fate of its kin, the remaining creature lunged at Knowles, its cry vehement and feral in its haste to draw blood.

But as powerful as the assailant was, Knowles was quicker. She managed to dive right as the Yeti surged towards her, the concentrated fire of the Glock and Hastings' carbine eating into the creatures head until it became a shapeless sac. The creature's body jittered like a faulty marionette before collapsing, its limbs trembling in an endless seizure.

Amid the fog of cave dust and gun smoke, Hastings and Knowles looked down at their strange foes, amazed and incredulous, despite the undeniable reality of it all.

Their reverie was broken by a distant cry, and despite the influence of chamber and tunnel, Hastings and Knowles recognised the ghostly echo as human.

'Johns?' Knowles questioned.

'It came from the chamber ahead,' Hastings said. 'Let's go. Double time.'

They moved, their faces grim with determination, the tunnels about them reverberating with an eerie blend of footfalls and distant, savage growls. *En route*, they checked on their weapons, primed them, making damn sure they weren't going to malfunction in the face of this brutally efficient enemy.

The silvery light intensified as they navigated a short tunnel, its arched ceiling a web of incandescent white veins, and reminiscent of a violent lightning storm. Beyond this a vast cavern opened out before them, the floor obscured by an undulating mist turned to cream by the ethereal light from the walls.

'Shit this is spooky,' Knowles said.

'Stay focused, marine,' Hastings said.

'I ain't a marine anymore,' she hissed. 'I'm a fucking window cleaner with a Glock 19.'

'Just keep shooting when I need you to,' Hastings said, edging forwards.

They moved further into the chamber, Knowles checking out a large stalagmite as thick as the trunk of a tree, mentally noting it as a landmark for when it was time to leave. *Ever the optimist, Knowles*, she thought. She smiled grimly to herself.

The ground beneath the smog - beneath their feet - was uneven, and each step was leading them into the unknown. Nearby they saw familiar shapes, mounds of fur lumbering through the ethereal landscape, tendrils of mist wavering about them like some ghastly spectre trying to drag them to their grave.

But these creatures had a supernatural aura of their own. These were the things of myth and legend, alive and indefatigable. Hastings and Knowles watched as they passed through chamber. They had purpose and determination with each giant stride. But also in the mist was another cry of pain from Johns.

'He's over on the left,' Hastings said back to Knowles.

She squinted and made out a shadow in the fog - a big man clutching at his head. The Yeti were also zeroing in, ten metres away and closing.

'Cover me,' Knowles said, and made for Johns before Hastings had time to protest.

He lay down suppressing fire, and the incoming beasts screamed in protest as one of their number went down, a cloud of rising fog marking his resting place. Knowles used the moment to close ground between her and Johns who was now on his knees clutching his head in both hands.

She knelt down as another creature towered over them. Her Glock spat two rounds, punching out its eyes, and sending it reeling into the mist.

'On your feet, Johns,' she said. 'We are leaving.'

'Something's wrong,' he grimaced.

'Fuck me. You noticed?'

'My head feels like it's gonna pop like a boil,' Johns explained. 'My fucking stomach hurts … real … bad.'

'Well, unless you get on your feet, I'm going to shoot you. Make a fucking choice, and make it now.'

Johns responded by standing up, his gait unsteady enough for Knowles to put an arm about his waist, and pulling his body towards her. It was like leaning against a wall.

Hastings was suddenly with them. He released two short bursts from the M4 into the next tunnel where several shadows recoiled with hideous whines and snarls.

'Move out,' he yelled. 'Johns, where's the transponder?'

Johns looked at Hastings, but his eyes were wild and confused.

'I can't remember,' he said. 'Did I have it? Did I …'

'We have to go,' Knowles said as another group of Yeti came into view. 'How many of these fuckers are there?'

'Too many,' Hastings said, checking over the M4. 'Swap, Knowles.'

Hastings handed her the rifle and took the Glock. He also took charge of Johns who was now muttering incoherently, his eyes vague.

'Take point,' he said, and Knowles got herself into position. They made their way carefully through the chamber,

Knowles keeping the exit tunnel in her sights, the M4 sweeping their approach, waiting to fire on any emerging target.

Given their size, even Knowles was taken off guard when a shape rose from the mist in front of her like the summit of a mountain through low cloud. Before she could react, a big, open palm had connected with her upper body and swiped her sideways, the M4 skittering off to places unseen.

Knowles disappeared into the low-lying fog, and despite the frantic cries of Hastings, did not resurface.

**

Hastings watched Knowles go down, his rage tempered by the terrible feeling of loss in his heart. In an attempt to get to his fallen comrade, he dragged Johns with him despite the moans of protest this brought from the other man. But no sooner had Hastings moved in on the spot where he had seen Knowles disappear, several other creatures were suddenly emerging from all areas of the chamber.

Hastings put two down with the Glock, but he cried out in frustration as more beasts took their place, the snarls and shrill screams of these feral, vicious animals now ripping through the air. With great reluctance, Hastings had to succumb to the reality that Knowles was gone, and there was nothing he could do but stay on mission.

Being in command was a bitch.

No, more than a bitch, it was a parasitic whore that sucked the emotion from the soul and kept it in its belly until dark and lonely nights, where it would spit the guilt and despair in your face, then gloat as you wore hopelessness like an ill-fitting blanket in guilt's brisk chill. Where it would take you to a place in which, even in the company of those you knew and cared for, you felt alien and alone, an outsider, divorced from a world that seemed more like make-believe.

But make-believe now had a whole new meaning. Nothing was supernatural anymore. It was now natural and super violent.

And it was coming for them through tunnels of frigid rock and eerie light.

With the chamber filling up with creatures, Hastings and Johns made for the exit tunnel, the mist about their feet a swirling and writhing afterglow, marking their passing.

'Quit fighting against me, Johns,' Hastings snapped. 'You want to get out of here or not?'

'I don't feel good,' Johns said. His voice sounded desperate. But above all he sounded afraid. 'I feel strange.'

'There's no time for it, you hear?' Hastings yelled as he increased the pace, yanking Johns along with him. 'Not sure what kind of outfits you're used to, but here we work for a living. And we sure as hell don't quit!'

They passed through the access tunnels and into the antechamber, the bright shafts of light directing them towards the cave exit. Snarls and growls were still at their backs, and as Hastings neared the cave entrance, he risked looking back.

To his surprise the pursuers, a group of at least ten creatures, were lurking in the tunnels, but making no attempt to move towards the daylight. They held paws up to shield their eyes.

'They're vulnerable to the daylight,' Hastings said. Incredulity as well as relief came with his statement.

He steadied his breathing and allowed Johns to do the same. On the threshold between the underworld and the Nepalese mountains, Hastings made some attempt to fathom what the fuck was going on.

***

'Motherfucker.'

In the chamber, Knowles sat up and rubbed at her head with a drawn-out sigh. There was a sizeable lump on her crown where she'd landed and hit it against a rock. Her right leg seemed to be at an odd angle, and there was a nagging, deep rooted ache in her shin. At ten-years-old, she'd fallen off her skateboard trying to do a Feather Flip, and fractured her fibula. Today the pain was the same. Today she had come off second best against a beast that had once been thought of as a figment of someone's imagination.

In reality, Knowles was more surprised by the fact that she was still alive. She remembered the blow, she remembered taking to the air like some half-arsed superhero, but the lights had gone out when she'd landed.

Knowles scanned her surroundings. The chamber was quiet and the floor-mist undisturbed. It seemed a far cry from the chaos that had preceded her trip to temporary oblivion. She had no sense of time so could not guess at how long she'd been out. The eerie glow from the rocks made sure the whole chamber was cast in a perpetual half-light.

Gingerly she reached down and checked out her injured leg, grimacing as her fingers made contact with her shin. Despite this, she probed the area, and was relieved to feel that there was no indication of bone protruding through the skin, meaning that the break was at least clean. She'd have to move it at some point. Though she figured that if she was still breathing then the creatures didn't know she was here. The shroud of fog was her only ally, and she needed to use it to the max.

She toyed with the idea that if she did a slow recce of the chamber she might come across the M4. She quickly told herself that more likely than not, she wouldn't find anything but false hope. As unsettling as this thought was, Knowles managed to swallow it, and move on to looking at the tunnels about her. She was now able to see that there were five exits. Yes, she could see the large stalagmite that marked the way out, but to the left of it was a second tunnel, and to her surprise and great sense of curiosity, there was a pulsating green glow emanating from the mouth.

'Shit, Knowles,' she said. 'You're not in any shape to go all *Sherlock* on current events. Get your fucking backside out of this hole.'

And this was her intention as she carefully dragged herself backwards, her backside sliding over the chamber floor, her head craned over her shoulder so that she could see where she was going.

But that was before the sinister growl came from a place to her left, and a great shadow fell across her.

Knowles looked up at the mountain of shaggy fur, the hand that was reaching down for her was open, fingers splayed, claws curved and glinting in the cave lights. A small hiss escaped from her lips, the only protest her terror could muster, as the thing standing over her gave out a cry of its own as its hand grabbed hold of her, and lifted her off of the floor.

As the beast brought Knowles' face into its own, and the cavernous maw opened to reveal its razor shape teeth, then - and only then - did Knowles find her scream.

***

Hastings helped Johns onto the shelf, his intention to create a harness from their rucksacks and a spool of guy rope in order to lower the big man down to the snow below. The wind was coming in from north, bringing with it a biting cold that had Hastings wrapping his scarf about his face before assisting Johns.

As he adjusted Johns' scarf, Hastings stalled when he saw the man's face. It was ashen, and the eyes were sunken into deep dark sockets. The skin about his nose and mouth appeared loose, as though the flesh was too big for the skull beneath it. Johns' blue-grey lips moved soundlessly as he allowed Hastings to secure his scarf and adjust his coat like a carer assisting an elderly relative.

Deep inside, Hastings was glad to be covering the sallow face with the swathes of fabric afforded by Johns' scarf. It filled him with revulsion, and if he were honest, created anxieties he usually kept at bay when on mission.

'Don't know what the fuck's going on,' Hastings said, 'but we got to get you out of here.'

'I'm scared,' Johns whispered through his scarf. His voice was a tiny thing to be whipped away by the bitter wind.

Hastings said nothing. Instead he prepared the harness, making sure it was fit for purpose, the knots expertly executed. He moved Johns onto a rectangle of thick material made from the ruck sack and tied the strapping across his waist, creating a makeshift seat.

Satisfied, Hastings pulled the walkie-talkie from his coat. He'd already tried it once before leaving the cave but was met only with a burst of electrical fizz. This time proved no different and with frustration he shoved the device back into his pockets.

'Looks like I'm on my own,' he muttered. As he prepared Johns for an ungainly descent, Hastings shoved away the thought that his last statement could not have been any further from the truth if he'd tied it to the hull NASA's Orion spacecraft. The things in the cave were still there; he could sense them lurking in their murky netherworld, biding their time.

Waiting for the darkness to return.

The thought of being caught on the slopes come nightfall was not filling him with optimism. He had to get back to the others and weigh the options. Knowles was gone, a fact he was still managing to keep under the lid, but it was a tenuous seal, and he suspected Appleby's son had probably succumbed to the same fate. Then there was Johns. Fuck knew what the hell was happening to him, but he was sick and needed treatment ASAP.

'Yeah,' Hastings said as he looped rope to the base of a tall stalagmite in the mouth of the cave. 'Makes sense to me. But will it to a father determined to find his son?'

Without answer, he secured the rope to Johns' harness, and moved him to a seated position so his charge could dangle his feet over the ledge. Johns was malleable, a giant automaton who allowed Hastings to manoeuvre him into position.

Hastings used his shoulders as a fulcrum for the guy rope, and then eased Johns over the lip, teeth clenching as he took the weight. Slowly and deliberately, with the rope creaking in the bitter wind around them, Hastings lowered Johns to temporary safety.

CHAPTER EIGHT

Appleby and Grace fought their way through the snow. In places, it came up to their thighs despite the protection afforded by the cliff face to their left. They had waited for the others to return, but Appleby had decided to make a decision based on urgency and need. The tracking device told him that something he held dear was only a kilometre away, the reaffirming bleeps thick in the still, crisp air.

Part of his mind considered recent events, the incredible possibility that the very creatures many had thought mere myth may well be a reality. It should have left him in awe, but instead he found the whole thing a distraction, an obstacle to locating and completing his goal.

Grace was ahead of him. He watched her moving through the snow, and not even her cat-like grace could prevent her appearing unsteady as she waded through one snow drift after another. All about them the northerly wind was like fire to the skin, and he adjusted his weatherproofing to neuter its bite.

Ahead was hope. But behind them, back at the camp, there was only carnage. It had to be this way because, as was so often the case in the murky world of subterfuge, things were not always exactly as they seemed.

***

Knowles screamed long and hard, the jaws of the terrible beast filling her vision. Like the frigid world outside the cave, her mind was frozen, a perpetual sense of arrest that helped her to come to terms with the enviable: that she was about to die a hideous and violent death. In some ways, she had always known it was to be this way; she was a soldier after all, and the gears of war were unforgiving. Perhaps it was the nature of her pending demise that made her suddenly pull free from accepting her fate, but whatever the reason, she found herself aware of movement beyond the jaws bearing down on her throat. A shadow rose behind the beast holding onto her, another creature, but this one was holding a twisted object, a crude club made from shimmering cave rock. The weapon was raised high and made a swooshing sound as it moved through the air and connected to the head of her would-be killer.

There was the terrible sound of something breaking, a sharp crack that echoed through the cave as the club buried itself deep into the creature's crown, slamming its mouth shut with such power, teeth shattered and flew into Knowles' face stinging her brow like shards of glass. Her assailant no longer had hold of her, and she was falling, the realisation coming shortly before she landed on her injured shin, and pain exploded through her leg, forcing a sickening cry to emerge from her lips. She toppled and lay on her side, the agony consuming her for a few moments before she opened her eyes and saw her attacker on its knees, head on its chest, its hands opening and closing as though trying to clutch at something unseen. Then the second creature moved into view, its eyes never leaving the fallen beast, the club bouncing in its hands as though it was testing its weight. Without warning, the club was swinging again, this time in a wide arc, and the cave was once again filled with the sickening crunch of rock hitting bone.

The creature on its knees was sent sideways, and the club finished its arc, the mist rising to accept it, the only evidence of its passing a shivering arm that rose from the grey sea, fingers splayed but now still.

Despite her pain, Knowles kept the Yeti with the club in sight, waiting for another assault. There was a fire in her belly, her desire to stay alive now that she had somehow managed to avoid death. As battered as she was, there was still a chance. The creature moved towards her, but there was something in its demeanour that was different. Rather than snarl and growl, the beast moved with silent caution, its shaggy head turning to one side then the other as it crept through the cave towards her. She saw something else. A wicked gash in the creatures slide seeped dark blood, but Knowles' concerns quickly returned to her own fate.

'Stay the fuck away from me!' she hissed. The pain gave her voice an edge, but rising fear softened it a little. To her surprise, the Yeti paused. Again, it scrutinised her with eyes of deep brown, its high forehead glistening under the sickly, silver light.

He took a careful step forward, the mist about its legs moving towards her in waves. Knowles shuffled backwards, and the pain in her leg was immediate. She gritted her teeth and whined pitifully. She found her back against the cave wall. She'd run out of places to go.

The creature stopped, and she looked back at it. Anger as well as fear was inside of her.

'Come on, then,' she said. 'Do your fucking worst. You hear me, you great hairy bastard?'

But what the creature did next confused as well as amazed her. It threw the club aside and held out its hands, palms up and open - a universal gesture of disarm.

'Oh, my god,' she whispered in awe. 'Are you trying to *communicate*?'

The Yeti knelt down so that it was at her level. Without taking its eyes off her, the creature adjusted itself so that it finally sat down, legs crossed and casual, elbows resting on knees, and fingers interlocked and supporting its bearded chin. The action was so human-like it left Knowles temporarily dumbstruck. Such was her nature, the silence did not last for long.

'So what now?' she said. 'We getting into a staring contest until I die of septicaemia?'

The creature remained vigilant, his eyes studying her from afar. Oddly, she began to relax though she remained alert. These were crazy days, and situations had a habit of changing by the second.

A few moments later the creature lifted one of its hands and extended a long black finger. It pointed at Knowles' leg. Then it brought up its other hand made two parallel fists, palms down, it twisted the hand downwards twice and Knowles could see that this great, incredible creature had made the gesture of snapping something. The beast understood that she had broken her leg and was able to communicate that to her!

'You're one smart son of a bitch,' she said. 'Yeah, I broke my leg.'

The Yeti pointed at himself and then at a spot next to her. She looked at him for a while before responding.

'You asking me if you can sit next to me, right?' she said. She sighed and nodded.

Carefully the beast eased itself onto all fours and slowly crawled over to her, its great bulk casting a shadow over Knowles the way a thunder cloud blackens the fields on a summer's day. After positioning itself next to her, the Yeti leaned back against the cave wall, and had anyone stumbled across them at that moment, they would have looked like two friends resting up after a hard day's work.

Knowles looked up at the Yeti. Its head was incredibly big, but those eyes held something else, something that, for a few seconds, she could not quite place, but then she had it. There was *empathy* there, pity of a sort, the way a parent looks at a small child that has tumbled over and grazed a knee.

'I'm guessing you ain't no ordinary animal,' Knowles said. 'You sure as hell ain't the same as those things that came at us in the tunnel. Makes me wonder what the hell is going on.'

The creature pulled a bemused face as though it was equally as baffled by the whole exchange, his expression made her think of the purple, hairy creature from Pixar's *Monsters Inc.* movie. She'd watched it countless times as a kid, and his quasi-human grin always made her feel happy.

'How about I call you *Sully?*' she said with a small smile which her unlikely companion copied.

This made Knowles chuckle despite her pain. And when the Yeti began to mimic the sound, she began to laugh harder making the creature guffaw in a series of short, snuffling grunts.

Then they both filled the cave with laughter.

***

Hastings unbridled Johns from the harness, leaving him slumped up against the base of the cliff. The man's legs buckled, and he slid down the wall until he was sitting in the snow, his clothing looking as if they belonged to someone twice his size.

Poor bastard is wasting away, Hastings thought. *But how? Why?*

It crossed his mind that perhaps Johns had been contaminated by something inside the cave. Then the quiet panic when he remembered he'd been in the cave, too. What if he was doomed to the same fate?

Subconsciously, his hands checked himself over while he assessed the route back to camp. He tried the radio again and was relieved when Appleby's voice came through the static.

'Hastings? Is that you?' the professor sounded relieved.

'Yes.'

'Thank God,' Appleby said. 'We've had trouble.'

'At least this mission's consistent,' Hastings said. 'I lost ...' he paused, fighting back a wave of grief. He continued, 'We lost Knowles. And Johns is sick. If he's got any chance of staying alive, we've got to get off of this mountain, Professor.'

'We can't,' Appleby said.

'I get your disappointment,' Hastings said. He paused and gained composure in order to press forward his argument. 'And you're right, I am a father, and I do understand. But we got trouble here the likes of which is beyond our experience. These things are real, Professor. I've seen them up close and pissed off. Lots of them. They killed Knowles. Come nightfall no one is going to get off this slope alive.'

'We can't leave,' Appleby said, his voice harsh through the static. 'Because Grace and I are trapped. One if those creatures attacked the camp. And we need you to come and get us.'

'Let me speak to Vine,' Hastings said.

There was sudden shouting in the background and a small cry of surprise.

Then the radio cut out. Any attempt to re-establish contact was met with the monotone hiss of static.

'Damn it,' Hastings spat as he went over to Johns, grabbing hold and yanking the resting man to his feet as Johns muttered incoherently into his face scarf.

'Yeah, I know,' Hastings said as he dragged Johns along with him. 'You know a mission has gone to shit when you, me, and a fucking Glock 19 constitute a backup plan.'

Hastings looked towards the direction of the camp, noticing the bulbous clouds rolling in from the north. By the time they were approaching what was left of the campsite; fat snowflakes were turning their lumbering figures into ghosts.

But even as he saw the distant, ragged tents being jostled by the breeze, Hastings' eyes were drawn to the crimson smear strewn across the campsite like a fresh wheal. The terrible sight made him push on, neither Johns nor the incoming blizzard diminishing his resolve until he got into the camp and witnessed the real horror what was waiting there for them.

***

Hastings found Vine's body eviscerated and left spread across the remnants of the tents: dark, crimson slurry that streaked out as far as the blizzard would allow Hastings to see.

For the first time on any mission, tears welled, his vision blurring and turned to headlight spangles by his yellowed goggles. Anger rose, and he clenched his gloved fists. He left Johns swaying like a tree in the growing wind, only the knee-deep snow keeping him upright.

Hastings stared at the bloody smudge in the snow, huge snowflakes settling upon the red crystals, making polka dot patterns, a token attempt to cover the tragedy. Vine's upper torso had been separated below the ribs. One arm was still attached, the other nowhere to be seen. The creatures had really done a number on him.

The radio in his pocket fizzed again, and he snatched at it.

'Appleby?' Hastings said. 'Talk to me, dammit!'

But it was Grace who replied. She was breathless.

Scared.

'We found something incredible,' she said.

'No shit?'

'A plane,' she said. 'A small jet on the slopes. We're holed up here. One of those things is outside.'

'Same thing that killed Vine?' Hastings growled.

There was a pause.

'He didn't stand a chance,' she said.

'You still armed?'

'I've got one full clip left,' she said.

'Then stay low,' he said. 'I'm coming to get you.'

***

In the cave, Sully made to stand up. He grunted, pausing as he leaned forward, and examined the wound in his side that was now a tacky smear.

'Looks like we're both pretty fucked up, big guy,' Knowles said as she saw the creature wince as he probed the wound.

Regardless, Sully stood and went over to one of the stalagmites rising through the ground-mist. One of his big paws balled into a fist and punched the rock, the stalagmite snapping with ease, and to the amazement of Knowles, allowed the silvery liquid inside to flow like a mercury-spill over the creature's fingers and into its palm. The liquor pooled like a shimmering lake touched by moonlight. Sully took the liquid and gently poured it into the wound. The fluid gave off steam as it made contact with the cut, and the creature's face was one of suppressed discomfort. But Knowles watched in amazement as the smoke cleared, and the gash was now a mere scabbed crust and all bleeding had stopped.

'Shit,' Knowles whispered. 'That stuff pisses on a fucking Band-aid.'

Sully held cupped hands under the silver cataract from stalagmite which had become a thin, sparkling stream. He turned and stood over her. He nodded towards her injured leg.

'Okay, big guy,' she said.

She removed her boot and gingerly rolled up her trousers to examine the damage, a manoeuvre that garnered many expletives, and hissed through clenched teeth. But the injury was sly, only mild swelling indicated that there was anything wrong.

Knowles looked at the creature's big expectant eyes, then her gaze fell to the silver liquor in its hands, and then down to her leg. She squeezed her eyes shut and nodded once.

'Do it,' she said.

She sensed movement, and then Sully's hand held her shin with a grip like a vice. Her hands went to her mouth, and the cry of pain was muted by the flesh of her palms.

The pain subsided after seconds, leaving behind a strange, aching sensation akin to a post-cramp muscle. She braced herself and pulled the leg towards her, surprised to find that a dull throbbing sensation was the only indication of injury. Tentatively, she stood up, her right leg taking the weight at first, but after a few moments, she tested the other.

The injured leg supported her weight. Yeah, she wasn't going to be able to run on it, but she could walk; a premise that only a few minutes ago would have been impossible to consider.

'The world ain't as I knew it,' she said as she put her boot back on. Sully bowed his head as though he understood. Knowles went over to the body of the creature that had attacked her. She pointed at it and then at Sully. She placed her own hand on her chest.

'Why?' she said. 'Why kill your own kind to save me?'

Sully's brow furrowed as he appeared to process her gestures. He nodded in understanding and went to the body and knelt down. His hands went to the corpse's abdomen. There was an awful tearing sound, and Knowles stared, perversely captivated as the creature's fingers sank into the thorax and prised the sternum and rib cage apart with a sickening crunch of bone cracking under great pressure.

Knowles expected blood, she expected guts glistening and slick with gore; she had seen enough carnage on the battlefield, after all.

But what she saw as Sully raised his hands and scooped out the beast's innards was worse.

Far worse.

CHAPTER NINE

Hastings saw the plane as he came to the crest of a small incline over several hundred metres beyond their camp. Below, a small valley had shielded the remnants of a Lear Jet from most of the blizzard, but its twisted fuselage remained submerged under a significant drift. The fat flakes falling from above drifted down in swirls and through this haze the tail fin and one buckled wing pointed towards the steel sky.

Hastings also saw the tracks. There were many, haphazard and carving deep trenches in the snow leading down the incline and into the valley. It was not lost on him that there was a pink hue to these tracks as the beast that had attacked Vine had been purged of spilled blood by virgin snow.

He felt grief rise but honed his rage, stamping it out. There were still people counting on him. Mourn the dead later; now was the time for protecting the living.

He could see the plane, but of Appleby and Grace there was no sign. Nor was there any indication that any Yeti was lurking outside. There was a moment of panicked assumption where Hastings found himself thinking that the creature was now inside the jet tearing Appleby and his daughter to pieces.

Behind him, Johns gave out a small moan, reminding Hastings of his presence. Things weren't looking too good for the big man. In the time that it had taken them to traverse the slope leading to the plane, Johns had become so weak he could barely stand. Yet such was the nature of his strange and current infection, Hastings had been able to half carry him as though he weighed nothing at all. Under his hands, Johns' bulky clothing moved and as it did so a soft sloshing sound, like that of a stomach filled with too much fluid, came to Hastings. He was left with the unsettling feeling that the man he carried was nothing more than a bag of sagging flesh, writhing and slithering at his touch.

At one point he feared his rough handling would tear the weak skin and pour Johns' innards out over the snow.

Yet, despite whatever pain he endured, Johns remained cooperative, allowing Hastings to assist him down the slope until they were less than ten metres from the entrance to the plane. Here he allowed Johns to sit beneath the buckled wing, sheltered from the snow now tumbling down like volcanic ash.

Hastings could see the entrance had been bent inwards and there were dark smears in the oval doorway. He inched forwards, his gun ready to put holes in anything that wasn't human.

He was about the climb into the plane when something came at him. The shape stepped out from behind the fuselage, rising like a spectre under the cover of swirling snow. His gun was slapped from his grasp. As Hastings gasped in surprise, another heavy blow to his temple sent him into darkness.

***

At first Knowles struggled to make sense of the thing that Sully had pulled from the abdomen of the felled Yeti. She had no reference point, just a large yellow sac filled with viscous, yellow liquid, which Sully broke open allowing a tide of piss-coloured water to pour to the floor.

She had a recollection: Hastings pumping bullets into the things in the chamber and the same yellow fluid pouring from the wounds. Those things weren't the same as Sully; this was made all the more evident in the hideous, yet incredible, creature Sully now held in his meaty hands.

Knowles moved closer to get a better look: it was a small, child-like effigy, two large fish eyes staring out at her, sparkling like highly polished glass, the large oval upon which these unblinking orbs sat, she now realised was a head on a stick-thin neck. Its flesh was a mottled purple-grey and pock-marked with deep, black pours that made her skin crawl.

'What the fuck is it?' she whispered.

But she knew.

Deep down her brain had retrieved the cave painting and processed the image of the hairy stick figures throwing spears at the avian object in the sky. Only it had never been a bird, had it? It had been an interpretation of something beyond primitive minds, and it was to be their demise, it seemed. Was Sully all that was left of his kind, she wondered. Did he now masquerade as one of them, ironically turning the tables on these incredible cuckoos?

Sully cast the small body aside and gestured for Knowles to look at the Yeti carcass on the chamber floor. She hobbled over and peered into the gaping hole in the torso. Inside she saw mechanisms and gears, laced together with fine webs of silver. This was a combat chassis, something to offer a degree of protection to the vulnerable entity nestled inside.

'How?' she said to Sully who looked at her, head to one side and shrugged his shoulders.

This bemused action gave Knowles an idea.

She reached down to the Yeti chassis and grabbed a handful of fur, and lifted the arm. It was heavy, the effort making her grunt. Then she tentative took hold of Sully's arm, mimicking his tilted head and shrugged shoulders.

'How?' she said again.

This time Sully's eyes widened with apparent understanding. He pointed towards another chamber, his head bobbing in the direction of the entrance, and lumbered off toward it. Knowles dropped the chassis arm and followed him.

Behind them they heard the sounds of movement; heavy footfalls of the pseudo beasts returning, she assumed, from their hunt for Hastings. Knowles hoped that her friends were still alive, and she fought against the powerful desire to leave the cave and go to them. But somehow she felt as though she could serve them better by being with Sully, to learn about him, and the things masquerading as his kin. It felt bigger, more important.

In terms of scale it certainly was bigger, in one day she had discovered the existence of a beast from folklore and the existence of extra-terrestrials. It was hard not to think she was trapped in a season finale of the fucking *X Files*!

Sully grunted with impatience and Knowles left her thoughts for a while.

'Yeah, yeah, keep your fur on,' she whispered. But it wasn't enough to satisfy Sully's impatience. He snaked an arm around her midriff and lifted her off of the floor, regardless of the brief shouts of surprise Knowles gave out as he yanked her with him.

She looked behind her and saw the large, haphazard shadows thrown about the chamber as the faux-Yeti emerged shortly after Sully lifted Knowles and disappeared into the opposite tunnel and out of sight.

Sully moved at pace, Knowles still coming to terms with the ease in which he'd lifted and carried her through this subterranean labyrinth. She put up a token resistance but whilst the arm about her waist was firm, it was also considerate; causing no discomfort.

They had gone several hundred metres into a complex tunnel network, the ever-present veins in the walls marking the way. Sully took one turn after another, but Knowles recognised a sense of purpose in him. The route was not random or reckless, and this was borne out by the images suddenly appearing on the tunnel walls, rough sketches akin to those she had seen with Hastings in the caves above.

These drawings were more detailed, and her eyes remained fixed on their intricacies even as Sully placed her down onto her feet. The images appeared as one continuous frieze stretching back along the tunnel for several yards. Sully grunted and she watched him move several feet away where he began to point at the wall. She walked over to him, her shin barely more than a dull arthritic ache, her eye widening as Sully's huge hand patted a painted image.

It was a scene of a Yeti family sitting in an archway which she presumed to be the cave. There were two other images; they were larger, and one had crudely drawn breasts, like something a delinquent school kid would draw on a toilet door in magic marker.

'I guess that's your mum, eh?' she whispered to herself. Her heart skipped a beat at the thought of her own mother. She forced herself to stay on target.

Sully pointed to one of the smaller figures then back to himself.

'That's you?' Knowles said. She emphasised by gesturing to Sully who bobbed up and down with a degree of excitement.

'I guess that's a *yes*.'

Sully then moved to another picture. It depicted him and his father carrying spears. There was a rough image of some kind of animal walking on all fours with horns pointing out of its head and a spear in its side with fat droplets of red blood falling from the wound. The next image showed the animal being carried back to the cave where it was spit roasted. There were several more images that told a simple story of primitive life as a Yeti, and Knowles followed these with rudimentary interest until she came to a painting similar to that she saw in the cave with Hastings.

But this time it was slightly different. This time there was a beam of yellow light streaking down from the bird-like image in the sky, and this light was striking the large Yeti - Sully's father. Knowles let out a small sigh when she saw that other paintings showed the creatures emerging from the machine, their big fish eyes drawn almost as big as their heads, the light beams cutting down Sully's mother and sibling. Instinctively Knowles' hand took hold of Sully's paw as he stood with his head down, lost in the grief these vivid memories brought with them.

'The world handed you a shit deal,' she said softly. 'How the hell did you last this long?'

But this was rhetoric; of course she knew. It was all there in the frieze. The expanded story of how this incredible creature, left alone after his family had been slaughtered by whatever this enemy from the sky was, how these things had used the bodies of his kin as a prototype to protect them from the elements, recreating them as vehicles to mitigate their own frailties once out in the open; how Sully had hidden amongst them, an incredible case of hiding in plain sight, irony on an almost iconic scale.

Knowles thought about the stories people had told in the past. Once they had been considered myth and the ramblings of the insane. Now she knew differently. Yes, some stories told of how people had been taken from the mountain by Yeti, never to be seen again. But if Sully was evidence of one thing, it was that these creatures were not savage monsters. They saw the value in co-existing with humans. Yes, they were shy and avoided confrontation, and Knowles didn't blame them in that respect.

She'd fought enough wars to know who the real savages were when it really came down to it. No, the thing that struck her most was that those who had disappeared had been taken not by Sully's kind; they had been abducted by these imposters. Johns had been the latest in a line of people felt to have been lost to the mountain. Perhaps Appleby's son and the team he was with were somewhere in these damn caves.

She shelved the reasons why they would do such a thing and mentally marked it 'for later'. The thing that made her do this was another thought that suddenly crept into her mind as she looked at the final image on the wall. It showed the craft that these creatures had arrived in, and Knowles looked at Sully and pointed to the painting.

'Where is it?' she said.

**

The world was suddenly grey fog. There was pain too; a dull and pulsating throbbing that left a semi-conscious Hastings with the relentless need to vomit. He dry heaved a few times, the pressure in his head increasing with the effort, making him groan.

'He's coming to.'

Hastings recognised the voice. It was Grace, and he fought to open his eyes despite the fire flashes going on in his skull. The images began to clear and he saw many things in quick succession, his mind churning as he fought to process them.

He was in the plane, the light coming through the windows was dull as though the sky was in sympathy with his circumstances, but it turned the jet's cabin into a place of monochrome shadows. As he exhaled, a delicate fog rose before him, the interior was cold, but not like the exposure of the slopes. The frigid air helped to bring him around, and he realised he was now sitting in a large leather chair. His goggles were gone, and his cheeks were tight with cold.

But when he tried to move, he found he could not lift his arms. Then he saw Grace sitting opposite. Her face was framed by the fur of her cagoule, goggles about her neck.

However, it was the Glock in her hand and pointing at his stomach that got Hasting's attention. It brought him out of his fugue, and he looked up at her. His eyes saw only cold distance - the eyes of a trained operative.

'What gives?' he said flatly.

She shrugged. 'Not for me to say.'

'You got a gun pointing at my guts. Step up a little,' he said.

'She's under orders.'

It was Appleby's voice that came to him this time. It was nearby, and Hastings winced as he turned his head to see the professor perched on the edge of a built-in sofa. He was holding a glass of scotch in a plastic tumbler, and he raised the drink.

'Great scotch,' he said. 'Though I did pass on the ice.'

'Want to tell me what the fuck is going on?' Hastings said. He moved his wrists, but they were held fast by seat belts lashing him to the chair rests. 'I thought we were trying to find your son?'

'What I was looking for was indeed very valuable to me. Far more valuable than a son I do not have.'

Hastings laughed. 'A double cross?' he said. 'Well, ain't I the sucker?'

'Oh, don't be too hard on yourself,' Appleby said. 'You're not as sharp as you used to be. You even said it yourself. Besides, I was kind of counting on it.'

Hastings turned to Grace.

'Guess you're not his daughter either?'

'Lover,' she said without hesitancy. 'Got a problem with that?'

'I got a problem with the gun,' Hastings said. He turned back to Appleby. 'So what were you looking for?'

'Don't need to look anymore,' Appleby said as he reached under his seat. He pulled out a small black tube with a shoulder strap. 'Found it right here.'

'And what you got there, Professor?' Hasting said. 'But I'm guessing you're not a professor either, right?'

'That part *is* true,' Appleby said. 'But I'm geologist, not an anthropologist.'

'You mean you know about rocks?'

'I love *stones*, Mr Hastings. Certain types of stones,' Appleby said. 'Diamonds, in fact.'

'In the pod?' Hastings said, nodding towards the container.

'In the pod,' Appleby said.

'Worth all the trouble?'

'One hundred million dollars,' Appleby said.

'That's a yes.'

'I guess you have a few questions?' Appleby said.

'You planning on killing me?' Hastings said.

'Yes,' Grace said.

'Nothing personal,' Appleby interjected.

'Shooting someone is pretty personal to the person being shot,' Hastings said.

'Perhaps,' Appleby said, and took a sip from his tumbler. His eyes closed as he swallowed the liquor; when opened them again he smiled, relaxing back in his seat.

'Well, this keeps getting more interesting by the minute,' Hastings sighed.

'I'll say,' Appleby said. He leaned forward, tumbler cupped in his hands, eyes bright with mischief. 'Want to hear a story?'

'Does it have a happy ending?'

'It does - for anyone who isn't you,' Appleby said.

Hastings' head turned from Appleby to Grace. The gun in her hand was rock steady, and the trigger finger was inside the guard. She could empty the clip into him in three seconds.

'So are you going to start talking or wait for the suspense to do the job of this Glock?' he said to Appleby.

'Where to start?' Appleby said. His face was one of amusement. Hastings felt the burning need to remove the professor's smirk with the butt of an assault rifle. 'When you have the level of prominence and funding I currently enjoy, Mr Hastings, you meet all sorts of people,' Appleby said. 'People of prominence, people of influence. You have grotty little pubs in squalid inner city backstreets. I frequent Gentlemen's Clubs in every major city on the planet. And gentlemen talk. They swap stories; they do business. You can pretty much get anything you want if the connections and the price is right. You are the scapegoat of this little ruse, no doubt about it. By the time they find what's left of you in spring, you'll just be another ex-marine that turned to crime in order to make ends meet.'

'You need a scapegoat?' Hastings said. 'So I'm guessing these rocks of yours aren't exactly kosher.'

'I made a significant investment in the product,' Appleby said, his tone clipped as though affronted. He paused to compose himself. 'And I have funded this retrieval mission. Perhaps this is what you might call compensation.'

Hastings chuckled.

'This is more than that and you know it,' he said to Appleby. 'I presume you got partners?'

Appleby's silence told him that his assumption was on the money.

'I'm also guessing they assume this plane is still missing,' he continued. 'And you saw an opportunity to make a killing. Literally in this case.'

'Diamonds are uncut and come from South Africa,' Appleby said. 'We intended to use the Nepalese/Chinese border; the Chinese uncut diamond trade is worth billions, a great place to fence stones in large quantities. But something happened. The plane lost altitude and came down here. I moved fast in a retrieval plan. All I needed was someone like you. People who were off the grid; people who wouldn't be missed.'

'And how did you find us?'

'As I've made clear, my estate is worth in excess of eight hundred million dollars, Mr Hastings. There's nothing I can't find once I put my mind to it. Grace knew of *The Sebs*, a legendary Black Ops team, now retired and off-grid. A few calls here, and few hundred thousand dollars there, and you people may as well have been wearing neon. So it's all academic once the wheel turns.

'As academic as killing us?' Hastings growled. He desperately wanted access to a weapon so he could shoot Appleby in the face there and then.

'I guess so,' Appleby said. 'Of course, I never counted on those creatures. It has been a week of surprises. I will return of course. There's a fortune to be made with those things.'

'What makes you think they'll let you get off of this mountain?' Hastings said. 'You got those things and *the believers* hunting you down.'

'The believers?' Appleby scoffed. 'They're as phoney as this whole mission. The people you shot were real police, albeit corrupt. The accident on the roadside was staged just to keep things moving along; to keep you all distracted. I planned it and made sure any witnesses were dealt with by you.'

'And the creatures?' Hastings said flatly. 'I'm no expert, but I don't think they're going to be up for being on the payroll.'

'I got a helicopter prepped out at Pokhara just waiting for my call,' Appleby said pulling a radio from his coat pocket. 'Unless those hairy bastards can fly, I think our odds are pretty good.'

The moments rolled out, and for the first time in as long as he could remember, Hastings was facing a gun. He wasn't so sure that this time he would be able to beat the bullet.

***

At the other end of the Lear Jet, Johns was consumed by his own war. But this campaign was being waged on a molecular level; out of sight of those too busy talking about diamonds and acts of betrayal.

The world about him was a surreal blend of purple and pink shades, the edges of the seats and fascia softened by a shimmering haze. Somewhere in what was left of his mind, Johns thought these images were quite beautiful, and it made his heart pulse, sending arterial blood coursing through him, feeding the thing that was rapidly becoming part of him.

He had no recollection as to when he had ceased to become human. Nor had he any level of understanding as to his role in this New Order. In reality, these thoughts were mere echoes, and secondary to his body's sense of purpose.

All he could do was slide into the kaleidoscopic world about him, and nature, such as it was, would be left to do the rest.

CHAPTER TEN

When Sully looked back at Knowles, his face was etched with confusion, and to her surprise, fear.

She tapped the image of the ship again on the tunnel wall.

'Come on,' she said softly. 'Where is this thing?'

Sully stood firm. Defiance exuded from him, and he rose to his full height. He was formidable, but there was also great vulnerability amid the pride. Knowles could sense this immediately. The great creature made to turn away as though he intended to move on without her.

'Wait up,' she called, and went after him. 'You can't just leave.'

Sully sighed, his melancholy palpable. He shook his head as though confirming some internal doubts and walked away, his hulking strides forcing Knowles to run to keep up. She ducked under his swinging arms and got ahead of him then stood there hands held up, a token gesture for him to stop.

He pulled up as Knowles breathed heavily. She was taking a risk being so confrontational, and she knew it. This creature could lose patience and swat her like she was an irritating insect on its arm. Yes, it may have had intelligence that made it more than a mere animal. But it was also living in hiding, fearful of the terrible doppelgangers now populating its home.

Knowles put her hand on the wall again. They were standing near the paintings that depicted the deaths of Sully's family. She traced the streaks of light coming from the bird ship. Her finger tapped the drawing of his father succumbing to the terrible ray of light.

'These things killed your family,' Knowles said as calmly as she could. 'If they leave this cave, they're a threat to my people. You understand?'

She followed this with flattening her hand and making soaring movements in the air to symbolise the ship taking flight. Sully's head tilted to one side as he took this in.

'No matter what happens, I have to make sure they can't leave this place,' she said. 'I have to make sure they can't hurt anyone else.'

She clenched her right hand into a fist and held it before the bird ship painting. Then she beat it down on the image.

'Time to take these fuckers out.'

Sully nodded again. This time his face was one of understanding and acceptance, all fear now eroded by a grim countenance that Knowles recognised as slow and brooding anger.

'That's right, Chief,' she said. 'Get into the zone. You're the only chance I got at saving the fucking world.' She thought this over for a few seconds and sighed. 'Can't believe I just said that. To a fucking Yeti, too. At least you ain't gonna be able to tell anyone, right?'

Sully made no commitment either way.

***

'So those creatures didn't kill Vine?' Hastings said. There was a cold anger in his voice.

'I'm afraid not,' Appleby said. 'I'm not sure who was more surprised, me when he caught us using the tracking device we said was with Johns, or Vine when I put two bullets into him. Still, it happened, and we had to make sure we got you here no matter what. So, we improvised with a hatchet. Or rather Grace did. She really is a naughty little imp when she puts her mind to it.'

Grace gave a humourless grin. The coldness in her eyes compensated for her beauty, making her appear both radiant and evil in one hit, like a terrible queen from a Grimm fairy tale.

'We had to stay on mission,' she said. 'You above all should understand that, Hastings.'

'You don't know what the fuck I understand,' Hastings spat. He was having a hard time keeping his anger in check. He wanted to end Appleby and his bitch so bad his hands were trembling.

'That may well be true,' Appleby said, 'but I knew that you had a part to play in all of this. You have to be on this plane to 'carry the can' as they say. By the time winter ends, there will be nothing left of Vine and Knowles. You'll be left here to become nothing more than a frozen corpse who died trying to take what didn't belong to you. Your team will be blamed for making off with the diamonds and leaving me and my fair maiden here with even more wealth that we already enjoy.'

'You better shoot me, Appleby,' Hastings said. 'Because I'm getting out of this chair once you're gone, and I'm coming for both of you. And I'm bringing my own hatchet, you hear me?'

'Shut up,' Grace said, and smacked him across the mouth with the Glock, chipping one of his incisors, and turning his mouth to bloody fire. He grunted with pain and blood oozed over his lips where it dangled off his chin as crimson threads.

'And I'm killing you first,' he said to Grace through lips that were already beginning to swell.

'Of course you will, big man,' she said dismissively. She stood up and went to Appleby who hefted the travel tube onto his right shoulder.

Seething yet helpless, all Hastings could do was watch the duplicitous couple make their way to the exit.

***

As they made their way through the cabin, Appleby paused to look back at his partner. Grace gave him a warm smile and kissed the professor on the cheek; the act was done with tenderness ambiguous to her recent, cold rebuff to Hastings.

But as well as being a creature of ambiguity, Grace was staunchly loyal. It was a trait she had inherited from her father, a gentleman who had kept her safe.

Her mother had left home when she was pre-school, and her father had given up a job at a university where he lectured in English. She was fortunate in that money was not his motivation; his gentle, erudite manner was galvanised by theoretical construct and debate. He also loved the natural spirit his daughter possessed; her ability to be carefree with a fierce sense of independence.

Somewhere between pre-school and sixteen years of age father lost control of daughter. But it was a quiet coup. There was no sudden going off of the rails, no drugs or booze or late night visits from the police. Instead, Grace's personality became somewhat skewed. Somewhere along the line, carefree spirit and fierce independence became selfishness and spite; a schism in which her ability to manipulate and always sate her own, ever-increasing needs became a priority. By the time she was eighteen years old, love was defined by what people gave her, be that materialistic or emotional, she was happy with either. That was not to say that she could not love, she could, but it was a variant of it, one that only came to fruition if all her needs were met.

Despite what she had told Hastings, Grace wasn't Special Forces, but she had fought secret wars. These were for people on government Blacklists and International Most Wanted bulletins.

As a mercenary, she learned pretty quickly that good money could be made and relationships kept shallow enough to avoid anything becoming other than business. When she landed a security job with Appleby, this was how it had all started out, heading his security detail, but as his faux-daughter, a relationship that worked for over four years without it becoming anything other than a commercial entity. And then she began to see traits of her father in him: his gentle, articulate manner, and the civility of his nature. Yes, she knew he was capable of making bad things happen to other people, but that didn't stop her feelings growing for him.

She fought against it for a long time, even convincing herself that anything she felt for him was a desire to have his wealth. But such ideas were quickly quashed, whenever she was alone with him, and she felt a level of contentment she only ever felt in the company of her father, and getting to the point that being away from him left her feeling empty.

Then there was the night of the National Geographic's Gala Dinner.

It was a grand event held at the London Savoy. She was wearing a flowing red gown, hair swept up from her slender neck, the halter collar exposing the pale skin of her shoulders. Appleby had stopped her leaving the back of the Bentley and placed a flat, velvet box in her lap.

'Something to complete the façade,' he said with a small smile.

'What is it?' she'd asked.

'Open it up, my dear,' he'd replied.

She popped the lid, and it had opened smoothly on delicate hinges. Despite herself, Grace had gasped at the incredible, sparkling necklace lying on a bed of white velvet.

'It's beautiful,' she'd whispered. 'I'll make sure I don't break it.'

'Do with it as you will,' he's replied. 'It is my gift to you, dear Grace. A small token of thanks for all you do for me.'

'But ...'

'Now, now,' he'd said. 'I will not hear any rebuttal. Yes, you work for me, but you never appear to want time off, and are at my beck and call every day. Loyalty reaps reward.'

'I'm not loyal because you pay me,' she had whispered. There had been a drawn out pause as she'd considered her next move. Then she decided to just say what she'd been thinking. 'I'm loyal because I'm in love with you.'

For a few awful moments Grace had been unable to read Appleby's face. Just at the point where she thought she had badly misjudged events, the professor gave her a small smile.

'Well, you have certainly left me speechless. And incredibly flattered, dear Grace.'

'Do you have any feelings for me?' she'd said tentatively. 'If I've crossed a line, sir, then you'll have my resignation in the morning. '

But Appleby had taken her hand in his and held it firmly.

'You will do no such thing,' he'd said softly. 'I would be honoured to accept your love. But to all about us you will still be my daughter. If you are able to accept this as a pre-requisite then I suggest we get you into that necklace and make you even more beautiful than you already are.'

Now, four years later and in the wrecked fuselage of a Lear Jet, Grace and her lover embraced, holding each other for a few moments, enjoying the contact. They stepped apart, and Grace looked ahead where Johns was lying propped against one of the walls.

'What are we going to do about Johns?' Grace asked.

'He cannot stay here,' Appleby said. 'It will spoil the illusion.'

'Yes,' she said, but there was sadness in her voice. Appleby patted her arm.

'I know he is a friend,' Appleby said quietly. 'But he is very sick. And we don't know what's wrong with him. We cannot take the risk of taking him with us.'

'You think it's contagious?' she said with some surprise.

'I'm saying that there is something significantly wrong with him, and it does not resemble any malady I have ever encountered,' Appleby said. 'If we take him away from this mountain it may put many other at risk. You understand this, yes?'

Grace nodded reluctantly.

'We shall take him outside before the helicopter arrives,' Appleby said. 'And do the *right thing*.'

'Surprised you guys have any concept of what the right thing actually is,' Hastings scoffed from his seat. 'If there's ever a convention for psychopaths in town, I'd put you down as a keynote speaker.'

'And maybe you can be the entertainment,' Grace sneered, 'as long as it involved violence.'

'Don't raise to the bait, dear Grace,' Appleby said. 'Mr Hastings is well past serving his purpose, and we must stay focused until the helicopter arrives.'

'How long?'

'An hour maximum,' Appleby said.

'Will they get through?' she said peering out at the snowstorm.

'The hourly rate I'm paying?' Appleby smiled. 'They'll get through.'

***

Sully steered Knowles towards a small recess several metres from the paintings. Here, he ducked low and squeezed through another opening that led into a small access tunnel that he had to navigate on all fours. Knowles followed on behind, her nose wrinkling as she moved within Sully's wake.

'If we're going to be partners, you think you could have a fucking bath at some point?' she muttered.

Ahead, Sully turned a corner and Knowles came up onto her knees as she navigated a cluster of stalagmites. As she followed Sully, she paused as the tunnel once again opened out into a large space that echoed with the distant sound of running water. To her amazement, the light flickered ahead as she saw a small cataract, flowing from an outlet high in the rock face and into a lagoon at one end of the chamber. The water was as cream and glowing with a white brilliance that almost dazzled her eyes.

Sully stood upright and made for the pool, checking periodically that Knowles was following him. As she got nearer to the water, Knowles smiled at the irony of her last comment as Sully stepped into the lagoon, sinking up to his waist.

'Want some soap?' she said. Sully looked at her blankly, and she giggled. 'This is one hell of a day.'

She dipped her fingers into the water, testing its temperature. It was warm and comfortable to the touch, but it felt thick - almost gelatinous. With caution she stepped into it, her clothing billowing out as she waded out to Sully who was pointing to the far side of the lagoon. Knowles could make out a bright portal and they started towards it, the water rippling about her.

They were halfway across the lagoon when she realised that they were not alone.

CHAPTER ELEVEN

The first creature rose from the water ten metres ahead; the second and third joined it seconds later, each emerging with a series of huge, gurgling bubbles that sucked and slurped as they burst like viscous blisters. While they had similar features, these aliens were bigger than their counterpart Sully had dragged from the fallen Yeti chassis. Their fish eyes were voluminous; their mottled bodies slick and shining as though coated in glycerine. But it was the weapons in their hands that become the focus of Knowles - long stems of dull metal with piping and bulked box-like structures at strategic points along the barrel. It was as Knowles marvelled at these creations that she saw one of the aliens lift the rifle and aim it at her. There was a low hum that escalated in pitch.She went left as a jagged blast of ARC light tore through the air.

Knowles was under the water as another rifle discharged, and from the fragile vantage point watched the brilliant beam waver overhead.

In her mind, the soldier was kicking in. She was unarmed and chances of evasion next to zero. She had the cover of the lagoon, but that was going to be temporary. Knowles also had Sully, but even with his great, brutal might, the odds still remained in favour of the enemy with their incredible *Arc Rifles*. There was another crackle of electrical discharge, more flickering brilliance that sent her diving deeper into the waters. She saw a drop off, the rocky ledge sloping off to a murky underworld, the colour of sour cream as the silver veins of light in the rocks fought for dominance. As she swam outwards, she saw frenzied movement to her right. An alien was diving down towards her, fish eyes gleaming, the Arc Rifle poised and ready to fire. Then he wasn't alone. A great mound of swirling fur was upon him, hands grabbing his neck, fingers probing those large eyes, a thumb finding an exposed iris, popping it, the alien's mouth opening and a small, shrill scream piercing Knowles' skull even under water. The Arc Rifle fell free of the alien's grasp as it tried to squirm out of Sully's grip, but the Yeti twisted with such force the head came off and green slime trailed lazily out from the stump of a neck.

As shocking as this was to Knowles, her eyes were already searching for the Arc Rifle that was drifting down into the depths of the lagoon. She could see it falling, a rod of silver twisting through the undulating water. A dull ache in her lungs told her that she was in need of air, but she kicked against it, her training taking her mind elsewhere, and she went deeper into the lagoon, her hands reaching for the weapon as it danced tantalisingly close to her outstretched fingers.

She snagged it as another pulse of light came towards her - under the water this time - and the blast was so close she felt the heat of it against her face. A huge muffled explosion bellowed out below her, a rising shroud of thick bubbles and rock rose up from the floor of the lagoon, the concussion driving her upwards, until she broke free of the water for a few seconds, using the time to drag in a huge lungful of air before gravity slapped her back into lagoon. She felt frustration at having lost the Arc Rifle eat away at her resolve, but this was only a temporary distraction as one of the alien creatures was suddenly under the water with her, staring eyes mere inches away. Its mouth opened to reveal a tiny aperture crowded with razor-sharp teeth into which she drove a boot, the heel caving in its face where its nose should have been. The head changed shape, deflating like a tired, post-party balloon. Green blood clouded its battered maw, and Knowles grabbed the Arc Rifle before it suffered the same fate as her recently lost prize.

Another Arc blast, another detonation, this time some distance away. There was a thrashing in the water; clouds of bubbles marking some great struggle. She surfaced to take on board more air, scanning the scene twenty yards away where Sully was using all of his skill to try and dodge salvos from the remaining alien.

'Okay, you bastard,' Knowles whispered as she raised the Arc Rifle. The stem had a small stock where her hand rested. Near her finger was a green stud. There were twisting pipes and bulky apparatus bolted both over and under the main shaft, a power source of some kind. But this assessment went through her mind in nanoseconds as she targeted the alien who, because of his determination to hit Sully, had not even noticed it was under threat until Knowles had discharged the rifle, sending a ragged arc of light across the lagoon and into its chest. There was a spectacular shower of sparks, and a fizzing green mist as alien blood evaporated under intense heat.

But extra-terrestrial muscles constricted in a reflex action that had the alien discharging its own Arc weapon as it spun in the water and, to Knowles' horror, the blast struck Sully, and brilliant sparks blossomed. Sully tumbled backwards, and the thick waters claimed him.

'Sully!' she called, and her nose wrinkled at the smell of singed fur and cordite.

Frantically Knowles searched for her unlikely companion, but there was no sign of him. There was a sense of panic as she realised that Sully had succumbed to the terrible Arc-blasts. Not only this, but she had to confess to a growing affinity with the creature, a lost soul in search of something more than their current existence. She waded deeper into the lagoon and, once more, called out his name, part of her feeling ridiculous that she was using a title she'd given to him, not expecting any response because of it. And she was right in as much as no one did respond, not Sully, not aliens. Just the sloshing water as she crossed the lagoon in search of her companion.

The glow from the aperture on the other side of the waters appeared to ripple, the resulting glint intensifying until it illuminated the cavern in great pulses. Knowles sank lower into the water until the surface tickled her top lip, and she watched as three more aliens emerged into the chamber. As with their colleagues, these were all brandishing Arc Rifles, and trained these on the lagoon as they splashed into the turgid surf. Knowles stayed as still as she could in the tide, the buoyancy provided by the liquid's strange composition helping her do this with ease. The Arc Rifle was aimed at the oncoming aliens, but as the creatures stooped to look into the waters about them, she sensed that she was not the focus of their search. This was confirmed a few seconds later when one of the aliens let out a shrill cry, and the others went to it. As one, the group scooped something with great mass out of the water, and Knowles knew in an instant that Sully was now in the hands of the very things that had murdered his parents and displaced his people. She looked for signs that he was moving, a glimmer that he was still alive. Then she saw a furry arm waving weakly as, with apparent ease, the aliens hoisted Sully into the air and carried him to the portal.

She was tempted to blast them all there, and then but strategically she knew this was a bad idea that would only lead to one fucked up mission. She needed to get through the doorway no matter what happened. Though she hated the thought of letting Sully encumber the enemy in order for her to gain tactical advantage, that was what she decided to do. As the group carried their prize into the shivering light, she swam beneath the water until a few feet before the shoreline then carefully surfaced.

The portal was a shining, oval slab which had now lost its intensity. Knowles assumed this meant it was closed to visitors. She climbed from the lagoon and cautiously approached the doorway. There were no obvious means to gain access, so she scoured the rocky doorframe for any sign of a handle or activation panel. Just when she was losing hope, her fingers happened across a small recess to her left. Inside this was an indent in which she planted her palm.

She felt the ledge depress, and the familiar pulsating light returned. Knowles checked over the alien rifle as though this was going to help her understand it any more than before. Then she pushed on the portal, and the next thing she knew the world had turned silver.

***

Appleby hadn't always been consumed by commerce. Nor had he always acquired his wealth through erroneous means. Son of Emily and Robert Appleby, two professors of archaeology working out of the London Museum, he had always been in the presence of the academic and the erudite. His upbringing had been nomadic as his parents globetrotted in search of ancient civilisations and cultures. And for a time, Appleby had shared their interest in this aspect of discovery. But that was before the trip that had changed everything for him.

His parents were at South Africa's Canteen Kopje, a world heritage site renowned for its stone artefacts, the barometer by which the traditions of man could be measured in millennia. But the area was renowned for something far more precious to some. The diamond companies were ripping apart the region in search of the stones for which man had a far greater appetite. All digs were fiercely protected for fear any of these stones were inadvertently discovered and removed. It was on one such occasion that a young Charles Appleby had been shown a small cluster of uncut diamonds by a porter he had befriended.

Appleby had been mesmerised by the find and insisted that the porter share one of the stones. When the porter refused, Appleby had run off with the stone he'd been given and promptly reported the porter who protested, accusing Appleby of being complicit. But an articulate British boy was always going to be believed over a South African porter. As the boy was led away by the police, Appleby had smiled to himself. He was the victor, and he had the spoils to prove it.

The diamond had been hidden away at their home in Hampshire beneath the floorboards of his bedroom in their large, detached town house; the prize was a tantalizing reminder of the things that were now fused: excitement of the discovery, and later - when he was older and got the diamond cut and polished - the beauty of the stones, as well as the thrill of almost being caught. They were the ultimate blueprint for a life spent in pursuit of perfection, whatever the cost.

There were plenty of others keen to make his acquaintance. His parents had always warned him of the criminal fraternity prevalent in the field of antiquities. The blood diamonds of Africa were only the beginning. As Appleby became more erudite, his choice of associates also enhanced. In university coffee shops, in the stuffy museum corridors, at huge gala dinners, the shadowy underworld wore the regalia of pious and upstanding society, but their hearts were always turned towards the material, the big houses in LA, the yachts berthed at Port Hercule, and the endless supply of cold, calculated cash. Just like the precious elements that he so often handled, this sense of omnipotence was to rub off on Appleby over the course of time. Eventually, it made him the man he was today: incredibly rich and with an intellect that was the only weapon required to stay ahead of the illicit game he played so well.

To top it all off he had Grace, of course. Her beauty was breath-taking; her physical prowess and drive equally so. In many ways she scared him. Not that he would admit to such a thing, but when he looked at her, watched the way she moved, the way she conducted herself about others, Appleby was as mesmerised by her as the precious stones he coveted so much. But she was also deadly, her poise as dangerous as it was elegant. It entrapped the weak, and she would always be ready to make people pay for their lack of foresight. Appleby never tired of her; he loved her more than he would ever admit to her or himself. Part of him was always ready to tell her, but another part, the part that enjoyed projecting the element of doubt into their affair, was never quite ready to come clean. Occasionally they made love, but it was not sought by either of them, it just seemed to happen. Whilst cuddling up after a candle-lit meal, watching the TV, or when they had perhaps had a little too much champagne at a charity dinner. And he enjoyed it, of course; she was supple and hard and eager once the gears began to turn. But months would pass before such things would happen again. It was their time together they valued more than anything, the secrets they shared that made them the perfect couple. Appleby had made it clear to Grace that she could seek out lovers of her own standing with his blessing. The rules were simple: she could have sex but not make love. That was the deal-breaker. That would be the end of it for both of them. He had told her this early on in their relationship, and to his surprise she had been mortified by the suggestion she could sleep with anyone else. It was there that Appleby witnessed her loyalty first hand, and it was this he ultimately fell in love with.

In his world, loyalty was as precious as the materials he moved around the globe.

'Hey, daydreamer. You going to help me or what?' Grace's voice came to him, and Appleby snapped out of his reverie.

She was standing over Johns, steam coming from her mouth as she spoke.

'Yes, dear,' Appleby said quietly. 'Of course.'

They knelt down and peered into Johns' face.

'Good Lord,' Appleby said as he saw the shrivelled skin about Johns' face and neck; his lips and eyes were grotesquely bloated, but the flesh of his cheeks had slid sideways like a cheap, oversized Halloween mask.

'What's happening to him?' Grace said. Her voice was firm but hesitant; the only clue that she was unnerved by Johns' condition.

'Your guess is as good as mine,' Appleby said. 'We'd best get him outside. Put this chap out of his misery once and for all.'

'I know it's the right thing to do, but it still doesn't feel right,' Grace said as she hooked her arms under Johns' shoulders. As she lifted him, his body felt as though it was a balloon filled with water. He had so little substance she feared he would come apart at her touch. Appleby took the man's legs.

'I understand,' he said softly. 'But there really isn't any other way. Look at him. Who knows the suffering he is enduring? This is the only option we have.'

'You guys are so full of shit,' Hastings called out to them from his cabin seat. 'This isn't about mercy. It's about convenience. Johns is a liability. You need him gone. Everything else is facia.'

'Ever the cynic, Mr Hastings,' Appleby said as both he and Grace lifted the unconscious Johns as if the action was effortless and began to carry him through the doorway. 'But there is little point changing a worldview five hours before you freeze to death. You lost your family based on an inability to belong. As endings go for loners, this is perfectly fitting. May you find the peace you're looking for before the lights go out.'

'Just keep looking over your shoulder, Appleby,' Hastings said. 'One day I'll be right behind you.'

'Optimism at last?' Appleby smirked. 'Maybe you will find redemption before death comes calling, after all. Goodbye, Mr Hastings.'

With that, Appleby and Grace took Johns out of the plane.

***

Knowles crept along corridors that appeared to be made of smooth steel. Her reflection was replicated from multiple angles creating a writhing mass of light and dark images to rival any carnival Hall of Mirrors she'd ever seen. It had taken some time to adjust to the environment once she had come through the portal. The air appeared a lot thinner, and rapid movement left her breathless. What she did notice almost immediately was a sequence of beaded lights in the metal floor that appeared to mark out directions.

The route separated into three different tunnels ahead, and as she walked across the pathway, the lights changed into different colours demarking individual routes. One of the routes was winking faster than the others, and Knowles found the intermittent purple pulse nauseating. Instinctively she fought against following this, but tactically her mind was deducting the design and purpose of this floor system, concluding pretty quickly that they were similar to a ship's emergency lighting helping to guide crew members at a point of crisis.

Knowles continued on her way, the purple pathway taking her towards the corridor on the left. Here the walls were imbued with thick bands of black tubing. She reached for one and withdrew her hand quickly because of the fierce heat radiating from its surface. Ahead, the corridor ended with a set of ellipses, making Knowles think of a figure of eight that had succumbed to exhaustion and fallen over. She approached the doorway, the Arc Rifle ready to dispense its deadly justice upon anything with fish eyes. The doors opened, and she dropped to one knee, the twinge in her shin reminding her that it still wasn't totally fit for duty. She held her breath, Arc Rifle steady and no-nonsense. But nothing came through the doors.

'Automatic,' she whispered with some relief.

She stood and peered inside at the space beyond. Another corridor, but this time it was narrow and its structure was that of yellowed glass. Knowles hesitated as she weighed up the composition of the corridor's shell. Then she stepped into it, and to her amazement felt as though she'd been thrown back in time. When she was eight years old, her mother had taken her to SeaWorld in Birmingham, and there Knowles had walked through a glass corridor beneath the tank and marvelled at the submarine world beyond the reinforced windows. But here there were no black tipped sharks, or manta-rays, no giant sea turtles.

Instead there was an army of Yeti.

Beyond the glass, in an open chamber surrounded by vivid, purple light, standing on galleys and walkways, upright and inert, endless lines of shaggy haired beasts, all of them with their chest opened, and even through the glass, Knowles could see the intricate mechanisms designed to house the alien pilots. The reclusive creatures of myth and legend had been bastardised into vehicles for their parasitic masters.

Anger flashed inside Knowles. Yes, Sully had already shown her that these vile creatures had made machines in the image of his kind. But she had no idea of the scale of their achievement. This was production line, the wholesale manufacture of …

'Of what?' she breathed.

She took time to look closer; pressed her face up against the window and scanned the walkways and the electronic paraphernalia they housed. Then she looked at a Yeti chassis that was currently moving below her, but it appeared different. There was something strapped to it, a harness - like a soldier's webbing. From this, a fat tank on its back and a larger version of an Arc Rifle – she figured an Arc-cannon of sorts - were coupled by a complex web of thin tubes.

Knowles scanned the rest of the chamber, and sure enough, there were many other Yeti machines wearing the same yokes; several of them were standing at attention and facing a circular hanger door. An alien creature was addressing them, its thin arms moving in the air. She watched as several creatures under the apparent instruction of their commander left the base through a small rectangular exit within the hanger door itself. She sensed urgency in their steps and wondered what it was that was driving them.

She forced her mind to focus. The gravity of what Knowles was witnessing threatened to overwhelm her. But when she considered the implications, all thoughts of Sully were placed on hold. Below, aliens had built vehicles armed with terrible weapons. From what she could see there were hundreds, if not thousands, of these devices. These were not a means to shield these beings from the vulnerabilities of life on Earth. They were machines of war, and the only enemy they had was humankind.

Knowles continued into the corridor and looked upwards to find that the ceiling was also opaque. Beyond the glass, Knowles could see beautiful cone structures of silver and gold suspended from a domed ceiling; these structures had a myriad of tiny lights twinkling like jewels at sequenced points from base to apex.

The cones were shimmering under her gaze, and from each of them pipes dangled like the tendrils of some aquatic beast, trailing away to crystal orbs of green light beneath the gangways.

'Power source,' she surmised.

As Knowles contemplated the scale of this revelation, she saw a group of creatures moving across a gangway below her. The aliens filed past another line of Yeti war machines suspended on cradles, a hoist underneath each armpit making them look like macabre, furry mannequins.

Her eyes were drawn to the figure the group of aliens carried, recognising it as the still unconscious Sully. It was with immediacy that she decided she needed to get down there to set him free before the aliens got to the rest of their kind. This was her opportunity; the advantage of surprise was all when you were outnumbered by the enemy. She made to walk along the glass corridor when she heard something shortly before the doors at the opposite end opened, and a group of aliens shambled onto the causeway.

The newcomers were communicating using a sequence of metallic clicks and short, sharp wheezes. It was a lilting sound made, not through their mouths, but small gill-like structures under their jaws. These strange articulations generated bizarre, drawn out tones, like a breeze moving across the vents of a giant church organ, and they were so engrossed in their conversation they didn't immediately see Knowles. The lack of awareness gave her time to lift the Arc Rifle. They saw her and stopped talking - stopped walking - and to Knowles the sudden silence was shocking.

'Put your hands in the air,' she hissed. There was a small pause and she shook her head. 'Did I *really* just say that?'

Knowles triggered her weapon and filled the corridor with fire. The aliens squealed as the beam punched through them, carving vicious wheals, showering the windows with sparks and thick wads of cooked, congealed blood.

One went for a pistol anchored to a belt shortly before Knowles removed his arm with another burst of terrible flame. Then the passageway was filled with only the acrid stink of seared flesh and acrid smoke.

Knowles navigated her way through the carnage, picking up a second Arc Rifle and the silver, angular pistol that the last alien had tried to pull on her before she severed its arm. She wiped the sticky green blood on the pistol grip on her trousers. At the doorway, she slapped her hand against a black square that had a small green stud at its centre. The door slid open, and she eased outside where an enclosed spiral stairway of webbed steel steps took her to the next level. Another door greeted her, another exit panel, but as she went through she was greeted by the incredible searing heat of Arc Rifle blasts.

The barrage sent her reeling back inside the stairway, hands and face stinging from the heat. She heard the escalating hum as many rifles charged up for another salvo.

At that moment, Knowles peeked around the door frame. She saw up to eight aliens, all armed with Arc Rifles. They were using the suspended Yeti war chassis for cover. Knowles also saw something else up ahead: Sully was lying on his back having being unceremoniously dumped on the gangway, enabling his captors to take up their defensive positions.

She could see the laboured rise and fall of his great chest, and his shoulder was a black mass of scorched fur. She felt a rage in her belly but tempered it, ducking back behind cover when another series of Arc blasts detonated against both the door frame and the staircase, the latter shuddering, its steps buckling under the onslaught.

Again Arc Rifles began the low-pitched hum of their charge cycle, and Knowles used the time to return fire. Her shot struck one of the Yeti war machines, blowing it from its cradle, and it fell onto one of the alien troopers, pinning it beneath a mountain of fur. One of its associates stood to open fire, and Knowles used the pistol to put a pencil-thin beam of bright blue through one of its bloated eyes. The creature went spinning into metal railings, cordoning off the edge of the gangway where gravity took its body over the guide rail and down to the hanger floor thirty feet below.

The other aliens were panicked and ran off back down the causeway where a bank of terminals and storage boxes provided stable cover. Behind the barricade a familiar oval portal shimmered, and through the gateway a huge shape emerged.

'Shit,' Knowles exclaimed as the Yeti war machine stepped onto the walkway. Knowles made for the junction box and hunkered down behind a knot of twisted pipes. From there she watched the oncoming machine, the Arc-cannon - bolted to the harness it wore - swept the causeway seeking out its target.

Her.

The machine stepped over Sully, and Knowles willed the Yeti to wake the fuck up and take the alien device out.

But there was no such reprieve; Sully remained incapacitated, and the alien threat was coming at her, Arc-cannon humming, the armour of its harness glinting as sickly purple starbursts. Suddenly the rifle and pistol, weapons that she had once thought incredible, appeared pathetic against the monster stomping towards her.

What she needed was some serious hardware; an MBT LAW anti-tank missile launcher would do the trick. No doubt about it. But from what she had seen on the causeway, there was nothing that could help her. In a few more seconds that thing was going to be upon her, Arc-cannon ready to fuse her to the metal floor.

Then she remembered the power source she had seen earlier; the silver and gold cones hanging from the ceiling. She looked up. Maybe she could use darkness as an ally.

'Time to put the lights out,' she said, and grabbed the Arc Rifle tight. She brought the weapon to bear on the nearest cone-shaped power cell, then sent a crackling burst of energy into it, not sure if the rifle would achieve anything at all against such an incredibly robust piece of architecture.

She need not have worried. The resulting explosion was massive.

CHAPTER TWELVE

Knowles' Arc Rifle managed to rupture the alien fuel cells, and the blast was loud and immediate. Two cones were severed from the structure and fell to the lower floor where they exploded, sending an expanding ball of violet flame across the hanger. Those aliens touched by the conflagration vaporised under the intense heat generated by the growing cloud, while fragments of metal punched through passageways, shattering glass. As the shockwave struck the bay doors, they buckled and flew outwards. Snow met heat, and the resulting steam created an eerie purple fog marking one world from another.

The concussion also made its mark on the causeway where Knowles was huddled away from the oncoming war machine. The whole walkway was lifted a few feet, and the squeal of buckling metal forced her eyes closed.   Fixings and railings also succumbed, and the Yeti war machine fought for balance on the now precarious surface. Its hands attempted to clutch a side rail that sheared off the causeway, almost toppling the machine in the process.

But somehow it stayed on its feet, and aimed the Arc-cannon towards her hiding place. Knowles rolled away just as successive blasts ate into the pipes and terminals about her, creating small explosions that, whilst pathetic in comparison to recent events, were no less deadly. Knowles came up to one knee, and another cone exploded overhead. This time it took out the access corridor, and glass rained down like purple jewels as the stairway twisted under the torque and pitched forwards several feet.

The gangway slewed, and Knowles lost grip of her Arc Rifle. She cried out in frustration and came up to her knees, grabbing a wrecked terminal to prevent herself being toppled off of the causeway. The Yeti was still coming for her; its shadow rose, towering above, Arc-cannon whirring as it charged for one final assault. For one moment, Knowles thought she could see its stomach roll as though the thing inside it was getting into a more comfortable position so it could enjoy the ride.

Knowles raised her pistol - it seemed a token gesture - she was out of time and she knew it. Her only hope was that she'd done enough to stem the extra-terrestrial threat or created enough of a ruckus so that someone somewhere, was now aware of their presence and coming to investigate.

The shadow of the beast fell upon her, and she closed her eyes. Some things were best left unseen.

***

Appleby and Grace lay Johns down on the ice. His frame was now so light they had easily managed to carry him two hundred metres from the plane to a small outcrop of rock with a hem of crisp snow. His breathing was slow, and at one point they both thought that he had slipped away as they were moving him.

The goggles on his face appeared to sink into his flesh, but when Grace tried to remove them, Johns surprised her by waving his arms and moaning in protest.

'It's the light,' Appleby said. 'He can't cope with it. Whatever illness this is, it's made him photosensitive.'

Grace nodded and left the goggles in situ. She pulled out her Glock; her countenance was grim as she looked down at the weapon.

'I'm sorry,' she whispered as she knelt beside Johns and placed the muzzle to his temple. Appleby stood behind with his gloved hand placed upon her shoulder. If Johns heard her, he gave no indication of it. He continued to move his lips soundlessly.

Before she could end his suffering, there was a dull thump beneath them, the surface of the landscape jolting, and sending clouds of snow several inches into the air.

'What was that?' Appleby said scanning the landscape.

'That was an explosion,' Grace said jumping to her feet, and stared up at the mountainside. A low rumbling sound came to them as they watched what appeared to be a cloud obscuring the slopes overhead.

'Oh my God!' Appleby said. 'Avalanche!'

With a lion's roar, the wall of displaced snow and ice powered down the side of the mountain, a churning maelstrom that gathered speed as gravity took it.

And below, exposed and helpless, Appleby and his lover could only watch it come.

***

Hastings struggled frantically against his bonds. He cursed at the effectiveness of Grace's constrictor knots, its figure of eight tightening as he introduced movement to his wrists. He wouldn't have expected anything less of her; it was clear she was a survivor, built to weather the ordeals of a *private security contractor*. The term made him smile; she was a mercenary, and her skills were not in doubt in his mind.

As much as he admired her, Hastings knew he would have to end her if he ever got out of the goddamn chair. Appleby with her. That they'd put his team in harm's way was all part of the job, but this was very different – not in the contract at all. Vine had been murdered and brutalised, Knowles had been killed in action, and it had been all for the sake of this, a ruse to cover the tracks of Appleby's nefarious antics and greed. Hastings tried to keep his anger in check.

Not too long ago this would not have been an issue. But now the years of enforced retirement had truly taken their toll, and he wondered if he'd made the call to take on this gig with his eyes wide open.

When he thought this way, he found that guilt was starting to eat its way into him, the influence his decisions had incurred on his team, on his ex-wife, and daughter. He cried out in frustration as the seatbelts dug deeper into his wrists and ankles.

Then he felt the thump beneath the plane.

The fuselage seemed to lift from the ground, and then landed, sending a shudder through the cabin. The plane continued to tremble, a distant roaring sound coming to him through the exit door, the din getting louder with each second. He leaned forward and peered through one of the windows and could make out a cloud of brilliant white bleeding through the twilight.

Hastings understood what was going on, the mountainside was disgorging snow. He'd seen enough nature and news shows in his time at the bedsit to know the potential power of this wave of snow and ice, the damage it could do to anything in its path. For once he was thankful he had the plane for some kind of protection, but he didn't rate its chances of staying put once the avalanche hit. He assessed that it would be carried on down the mountain towards the base camps, and the jagged rocks that would be waiting there. It was a shit storm, literally.

All he could to was to wait and ride it out, and hope that by the time it was all over he was still alive.

***

The war machine raised its Arc-cannon; Knowles hearing the incessant high pitched bleeping indicating it was primed and ready to blast her into oblivion. In that second, she made the decision to face her demise, opening her eyes and staring down the simian face, pseudo-lips pulled back, and baring its teeth like a state of the art animatronic in a movie. There were more explosions, but they seemed blunted by the enormity of her fate, to die at the hands of an awful yet fantastic piece of hardware, fusing inner and outer world in one brutal act.

There was another explosion from the ground level; violet flames blossomed and sheets of metal flew like aluminium foil on the super-heated breeze. The platform jarred, and again everything shifted, including the alien machine. The Arc-cannon sent a searing bolt of light into the stairway beyond Knowles, removing a panel of metal the size of a pool table. Knowles felt the heat of the beam as it passed over her head; she instinctively triggered the pistol and it splashed small sparks on the belly of the beast. It was insignificant enough for her to see how fruitless her weapon was against her foe, but it made her feel as though she was still fighting, still trying to show these things that no matter what they gave, she would still be battling against them to her last breath. She smiled grimly at the thought of being a symbol, an unedifying statement of the human condition, a statement that said: *'If you want what's ours, you'd better be prepared to fight to the last silver-bastard you can muster'*.

It was as her smile turned to a low chuckle that something quite miraculous occurred. The alien machine composed itself, widening its stance on the causeway so it did not fall; it primed the Arc-cannon, aimed, but never got the chance to deliver another salvo. A great, hairy arm latched around its neck, baring its windpipe, and dragging it backwards. The cannon sent an Arc-blast skywards where it blew a hole in the ceiling, and a cataract of rocks began to tumble into the hanger.

Then the snarling face of Sully appeared over the war machine's shoulder. The Yeti's mouth clamped down on the side of the machine's neck and ripped the head away from its shoulders. Gouts of dark goo splattered Sully's face and fur, and Knowles now recognised this substance as some kind of lubricant similar to motor oil, and equally vital to the functioning of the machine.

Knowles jumped up and punched the air.

'Sully, you great hairy bastard! I knew you'd get back into it! I knew it!'

Sully turned the battered war machine around and drove a fist into its stomach. There was a loud pop and a hiss, and the satisfying thin scream of the pilot as it was dragged from the carcass and thrown onto the platform. Sully raised a big foot and stamped the life out of the shivering creature.

Other Arc-cannons opened up, the explosions adding to the existing hell on the platform, and Knowles watched as a further two war machines scrambled across the platform. She recognised that the aliens that had taken cover had used the distraction provided by the chaos to suit up and join the fray.

Sully stood before them, one arm, hanging limply from the injury sustained at the lagoon. But in his other hand he brandished a length of twisted steel pipe, a replacement for his rock club, and as the Arc-cannons began their charging cycle, Sully leapt at the war machines, his makeshift mace swinging mercilessly.

The first blow took out the Arc-cannon on the machine to his left; there was a series of tiny staccato clicks before a small blaze swept over the harness, the flames quickly igniting the fur. In seconds there was nothing more than a walking sheet of flame that staggered about the platform until it stepped into the open air and fell, a smoke stream marking its descent.

The second machine punched out, the blow connecting to the side of Sully's head. The great beast staggered to the edge of the causeway, the flimsy rail barely containing the impact. The rail bent outwards and then sheared off, Sully going over the edge as Knowles let go a scream of rage.

Sully used his good hand to snag the edge of the platform and hang there, his cry of pain and anger so loud it rose above the chaos around them. The remaining machine took its chance and stood over Sully as it lifted a foot to kick him off of the causeway. Knowles saw its intention and charged, her small pistol pumping Arc-blasts into the fur where flowering sparks turned the hair into gaudy shades of yellow.

Although the assault had seemed to be token, it was not exactly ineffectual. The alien machine was distracted by her, turning its attention away from ploughing its foot into Sully's upturned face and sending him to the hanger floor.

The Arc-cannon arched, and then released a shot of brilliant light that had Knowles diving to her belly. The machine stomped over to her, reaching down in an attempt to grab and crush her between its automated hands.

Knowles scuttled forwards on her stomach and went through the machine's legs, rising when she was behind it, and facing the cylindrical power pack strapped to its back. She leapt at the device and yanked at the tubes and pipes fuelling the Arc-cannon; sparks flew and the whole pack began to shudder.

'That's not good,' she muttered as the machine spun around in apparent panic, dislodging Knowles who rolled behind a stack of fallen debris. She watched as the power cell erupted, cleaving the machine in two, splashing lubricant and alien blood across the concourse.

Knowles saw Sully as he struggled to pull himself back into the concourse. She went to help him, grabbing some fallen tubing and feeding it under his injured limb, reaching down to lash it across his back, then under the shoulder of his good arm. She took the slack and used one of the terminals opposite as a fulcrum, bracing against the machinery with one foot, and heaving on the tubing with all her might.

Sully's fingers sought purchase, and with the torque provided by Knowles, he hauled himself up onto the platform. Knowles came to him, both were gasping for breath, and as detonations and fire swirled in the hanger below, they hugged each other like long lost friends.

Knowles disengaged and pointed at the oval doorway at the other end of the concourse. Sully nodded that he understood. They headed towards it, Sully picking up his length of twisted pipe; Knowles recovered an Arc Rifle from the debris.

She primed the weapon as a shadow wavered in the watery light, and Knowles put an Arc-blast through the door. There was a screech as a lurking alien trooper was torn apart.

They entered the next chamber and paused for a few seconds, taking in the scene before them. The room was circular, at its epicentre was a great chair fashioned from glittering white metal, and its shape reminded Knowles of a tulip, her mother's favourite flower from what seemed like a lifetime ago.

There was another alien sitting in the chair, but its body was unlike its smaller counterparts. It had a large head supported by a neck-brace built into the seat, and its belly was distended like that of a woman in the third trimester of pregnancy. The legs were thick like the trunks of a mighty oak, and Knowles guessed that if this creature were to stand, it would almost certainly tower over Sully.

But the thing in the seat would not be standing anytime soon. The room had taken significant damage from the blast on the floor below. Overhead there were banks of oval monitors, their screens shattered and fizzing sparks or flickering with static. Some had fallen to the floor where they lay shattered. Several had collapsed onto the creature in the chair, crushing it where it sat.

An alien trooper scrambled through the debris, and Knowles took him down with the Arc Rifle before he had a chance to strike up a defensive position. Another man an attempt to use a machete made from a black material, the edges of which shimmered like silver fire. Sully dodged the blade as it sought out his chest, then smashed the pipe into the alien so hard it lifted from the ground and landed several feet away, an Arc of green blood marking its trajectory.

Knowles went through the chamber, fascinated by its structure. It was becoming clear that this was not a base carved into the mountain. This entire structure was the very ship that had landed here god-knew-when. The creature in the seat was its pilot, and they were now traversing what was left of the bridge.

If her assessment was correct, then she knew that they had done enough to cripple the spacecraft. These things weren't going anywhere. This meant, if she could get word to the outside, an airstrike could bury these fuckers in the rock for good.

At the other end of the room, Knowles saw an exit. It was a tall door, a slab of metal reflecting the fires scattered about the bridge. On their approach, the door activated, and slid smoothly to one side where a brace of moving pavements sloped off down towards the hanger.

Sully needed some encouragement to step onto the moving floor. At one point he attempted to beat it with the steel pipe, and only Knowles stepping onto the floor placated his suspicion of the alien technology.

As they made their descent, a wave of heat came at them through the opening below. Knowles could see firsthand the pandemonium taking place in the hanger beyond.

The icy blasts of wind fanned the violet flames that had sprung up after the power cells had erupted. Here and there, shattered remnants of the cone structures could be seen, sparkling in the garish light. There were Yeti war machines, too. They were either cast aside, heaped up against walls warped by the initial explosion, or burning brightly as their innards succumbed to the intense heat.

There was a loud and terrible screech, and the structure housing the causeway where Knowles and Sully had fought for their lives folded, the whole structure slamming down onto the hanger deck, sending a tide of pseudo-Yeti carcasses skittering across the smooth steel floor. The fur ignited as soon as the heat took hold, and the blaze burned so brightly Knowles had to turn away from its intensity.

Knowles tugged at Sully's good arm and pointed at the ruined doors marking the hanger exit. Snow gusted in through huge fissures created by the detonating fuel cells. The frigid air hit them, and Knowles pulled her coat about her despite the high temperature at her back. She yanked the goggles hanging from her neck onto her face.

'We have to go,' she called to Sully.

From deep inside the hanger came another massive explosion, and more of the ceiling caved in, colossal boulders smashed into the alien structures below, bringing about more blasts and destruction.

'Out there,' she yelled, pointing to the blizzard outside. 'We have to go before this whole place collapses on us.'

She headed out, and Sully came after her, the wind tousling his fur. The clouds were still rolling in from the north bringing with them fresh snow and the ominous darkness of the evening.

Knowles found herself exposed to the elements despite her weatherproofed coat. She shivered violently, and her teeth chattered as she looked up at Sully.

'Gonna be an ice cube in about forty minutes, big guy,' she said with a jittery smile. Sully saw her trembling and surprised her by stepping back into the hanger. He went left, disappearing from her viewpoint.

'Hey!' she yelled. 'Get back here!'

But Sully was nowhere to be seen for a few minutes. At one point Knowles felt she had little choice but to follow him into the hanger. The freezing cold was partial motivation. Just as it seemed the only option Sully stepped outside again. In his hands he carried a brown pelt, fur he'd ripped from one of the alien Yeti carcasses. He wrapped this about Knowles, and she sighed at its immediate comfort.

'Giving a girl presents is not gonna be good for your bad boy image, fella.' She grinned up at him. But Sully shrugged, showing her that he really had no idea what she was saying.

Through the hanger doors they watched as the rocks poured through the ceiling as the mountain reclaimed the space occupied by its uninvited guests. More detonations marked the death of this quiet invasion, and Knowles realised that her mission was done.

She shouted above the wind, making Sully aware that she needed to descend, gesturing towards the base of the mountain. He nodded, and led the way for her, kicking a trench through the snow that she followed with ease.

It was as she got to the bottom of the slope that events took an unexpected turn, and Knowles realised that strange things were far from over.

CHAPTER THIRTEEN

The avalanche careened down the mountain at over eighty miles per hour, the churning snow creating its own undulating mass. Like great waves breaking against the shoreline, ice and snow exploded as it hit the base of the rock face, sending a huge white plume skywards before the main waves surged forwards and out onto the plateau where it smashed into the Lear Jet, shoving the fuselage along for over two hundred yards before the plane succumbed to the inertia and rolled over, wings snapping off, its body breaking in two.

Inside, Hastings was trapped in a world of noise and violent movement. Somewhere along the way the chair to which he was tethered came free of its fixings, and he was pitched forward, his face planting into the seat opposite before he bounced backwards, the chair upended and landing on its back with a sharp crack. Hastings found his hands free just as the whole fuselage rolled, and his body coupled to the walls, then the ceiling, and then back to the floor where he lay winded and bloody as the bulkhead gave in to the abuse being inflicted upon it and split open like a cracker yanked apart at a Christmas dining table. Snow and the howling gale joined in with the cacophony that heralded the plane's demise, the brisk air biting into Hasting's exposed flesh, bringing him round with a small groan.

He opened his eyes and saw the wreckage scattered about him, and he could see a gloomy world of swirling snow through a ragged oval where the fuselage had snapped in two, the jagged edges framing the scene making him feel as though he was in the throat of some large beast that was trying to force him down its gullet.

Hastings tried to stand and found that he was tangled in the debris of the chair to which he'd been bound. His joints ached; his neck was a dull fire at the base of his skull, the slow pulse of whiplash beginning to assert itself. He tested his legs; they supported his weight, and there was no sign of broken bones. For the first time in some months, he considered himself lucky. And his good fortune would mean something quite different to the likes of Appleby and his psychotic girlfriend. Hastings wondered if fate had cut the bastards some slack, and they were currently lying crushed under plane or snow.

The gunshot and subsequent bullet that whined past his head sending him diving for cover told him that his kind of luck was returning from its mini-break. Another gunshot put a hole into the fuselage near to his arm, sending shards of plastic into his hand, making it wet with blood.

Grace was silhouetted in the ragged opening. Her Glock held firm in both hands. Appleby was nowhere to be seen, and Hastings had to assume the older guy was moving to outflank him.

'Get out here!' Grace yelled.

'No, thanks,' he replied. 'I'm pretty good back here. How about you put the gun down and come and have a chat about how we move forward on this business arrangement of ours?'

She laughed, but it was as cold as the wind pummelling the side of the plane.

'I think that time is at an end,' she said. 'Better to terminate the contract. Nice and clean, you know?'

'You mean no mess for you guys to explain away,' Hastings said as he adjusted his position so that he could peer over the top of a seat that was still in situ.

'There is that, I guess,' she admitted. 'But this is bigger than us. And it really isn't my call.'

'No,' said a voice across from Hastings. He turned his head to see Appleby through a portal to his right, gun aimed and ready. The older man's face was grim. 'The call is mine.'

The Glock in his hand quivered, but even Hastings knew it was pretty much impossible to miss at this close range no matter how fast he moved. Even if he evaded Appleby's bullet, he was pretty sure Grace would make sure of the job instead.

'I think I might be fucked,' Hastings said with some resignation.

'I think you might be right,' Appleby said.

Then he pulled the trigger.

***

The avalanche had brought thousands of tons snow down the mountainside. It had also uprooted plants and loose rocks, turning them all into deadly missiles as it pounded the slopes in a bid to be free.

But not only did it bring things of nature, this colossal, twisting maelstrom brought the *unworldly*, a platoon of great, furred war machines that used alien technology to not only ride out the storm but ride within it, gyros keeping them above the ground, their thick pelt protecting them from the sly debris peppering their coats.

These great devices alighted from the avalanche before it ploughed into the ground at the base of the mountain where it was to begin its slide into the Lear Jet. These machines watched from the gloom as the ice and snow rose like steam, and they used this natural fog as cover to group and march towards the plane, their mission clear - search and rescue. One of their numbers was in danger, and they would be the only means by which it would survive.

One of the machines - a huge grey-brown Yeti - led the hike. Inside, the pilot was honing in on the signal coming several hundred yards beyond the human aircraft. This area was now a clearing just out of range of the avalanche's reach. One of the other pilots crackled inside their leader's skull. A frantic, psychic cacophony informing all that their base of operations was now under siege and nearing destruction.

The thing inside the machine was used to shifting parameters of a mission. This was not its first incursion on another world. There had been many more. But the mission was always the same: infiltrate and embed. The processes were always long, drawn out, but it mattered not for a race of beings such as this. One year was a mere moment compared to their understanding of time. Centuries were how they measured a lifespan; millennia a lifetime.

The alien commander located their target; an inert Johns was lying as a lone shadow on the ice plain. But these things were not concerned with the state of the creature lying on the snow. Their focus was what it harboured.

Because, like the machines that played host to the aliens inside them, so human beings also served for the benefits of subterfuge.

***

When Appleby's weapon failed to fire, both men stared at one another in bemusement. Appleby squeezed the trigger again, and the staccato clicks were as loud as they were ineffectual.

'Guess one of us finally got lucky,' Hastings said as he launched himself at the portal, and grabbed hold of Appleby's arm. Grace opened fire from the other end of the plane, the bullets trying to seek out a target that was quickly becoming lost to the gloom.

Appleby cried out in frustration as he struggled to free his arm from Hastings' grasp, but to no avail. Instead, Hastings kept the arm straight, trapping it against the portal's frame and then powered forward. The elbow shattered as the arm folded against the fuselage, the crack only muted by the scream of agony Appleby gave out.

'Charles!' Grace cried out.

Approaching footfalls told Hastings that she was heading in to improve the odds of getting off a better shot. He wrestled the gun free of Appleby's mitt as Grace opened fire.

Bullets chewed into the walls, but one ricocheted and punched a hole in Appleby's face, shattering his goggles, and caving in his cheekbones. Blood flew as the professor collapsed from view, and as he went down his fractured arm was dragged through the portal like an escaping serpent.

Hastings dived for cover, pumping the Glock to clear the jam.

Grace yelled out, distraught as she realised what had happened. Hastings watched as she appeared to dither; he assumed she'd contemplated going outside to Appleby, but her rage appeared to give her greater purpose. In the half-light she advanced and came into view, her face twisted into a hideous mask of grief and fury.

'Look what you made me do!' she screamed. 'You've taken everything! God damn you!'

'*He* already has,' Hastings said raising his gun. Grace's eyes widened with realisation that her adversary was no longer unarmed. In her eyes, resignation appeared to stay for a few seconds then she braced to fire.

Hastings got there first - twice in quick succession - but Grace was dead before the bullets came anywhere near her. In fact, her upper torso was torn to pieces in a wave of terrible fire, her head falling into her pelvis with a slopping sound before her legs gave way and this macabre effigy fell to the deck.

He watched the dreadful shape entering the cabin, the shaggy hair silhouetted against the snow, the terrible Arc-weapon it carried glowing in the murky light.

Hastings reached for Grace's fallen Glock. Another blast from the Arc Rifle took out the sofa opposite, putting another hole into the jet's already abused body, and snowflakes blustered into through the gap.

A low-pitched whine emerged as the weapon began its re-charge cycle, and thinking that he had pretty much nothing to lose, Hastings stood and unleashed a barrage from both pistols, putting three bullets into the beast's head, another two into its gut.

The thing staggered back with an unearthly squawk and went down heavily, the rifle clattering onto the deck. Hastings moved, seizing the moment to grasp the weapon and try to make sense of it. Once he found the trigger, his mind was accepting that this was like any other weapon; as long as the dangerous end was facing what you needed to kill then everything else was downhill.

There were more shapes outside; the fuselage was buffeted by heavy thumps as more of the Yeti steadied themselves against the plane. A simian face appeared in one of the windows, and Hastings let loose with the Arc Rifle, a movement that was instinctive, and the weapon responding accordingly. The Arc-blast punched through the window and the face disintegrated, the fur about the shoulders catching fire before a small detonation slapped its innards against the plane's hull.

Hastings watched the swirling snow outside the fuselage, the darkness, the oncoming blizzard, were preferable to being trapped inside the plane with these deadly, incredible enemies. He edged forwards, the Arc Rifle now powered and ready to unleash its brutal Arc-blast on anything that moved.

By the time he got to the end of the plane, his world had turned to fire.

***

Knowles watched helplessly as the commanding war machine raised the Arc-cannon and aimed it at the man emerging from the wrecked plane. She recognised the gait immediately; she'd know Hastings anywhere, even in these strange circumstances, and she yelled out a warning just as the Arc-cannon spat fire.

Her words were whipped away by the wind, but the Arc-blast was undeterred, cutting through the falling snowflakes, turning them to steam, and striking the ground mere feet away from Hastings. There was a huge conflagration; fire punched skywards for a brief second before being bent over by the wind, and Knowles saw Hastings thrown into the air, his body bent and broken, firefly patches on his clothing winking out like dying stars. He landed several feet away from the plane.

'No!' Knowles screamed, and fought through the snow to get to the plane. She found herself scooped off of the ground as Sully came to her aid. They traversed the slope, Sully moving to the edges where most of the snow had funnelled down into the base of the mountain, and leaving their path moderately clear. The going was still arduous, but it took Sully minutes to get down to the crash site.

To Hastings.

The war machines had moved on beyond the plane and could not be seen in the swirling snowfall. Sully placed Knowles down beside Hastings. She found him barely alive. His lips were moving, the only indication that he was still conscious. His body was misshapen, and the snow was settling upon him as though trying to cover his terrible injuries.

'Shit, Chief,' she said as she leaned over him. 'Is this a good time to tell you I told you so?'

'Appleby,' Hastings muttered. There was blood coming out of his mouth as he spoke.

'Appleby?'

'Diamonds,' he said. 'All about diamonds.'

'Look,' she said, gently placing her hand on him. 'We need to get you out of here. Fuck knows how, but we've got to try. That's what *The Sebs* do, right?'

'Not this time,' he said. 'Just you left now.'

'Vine's dead?' Knowles asked. Her tears were misting up the inside of her goggles. Somehow it felt better to see the world this way; it made things seem unreal, a falsehood that she could somehow ignore.

'You have to go,' Hastings said desperately. He tried to lift his head, but ended up coughing thick blood down his chin where gore met the cold wind and turned to dark, sparkling slurry.

'Helicopter. Coming,' he eventually gasped. 'Appleby's crew. Take them out. Get the hell out of here.'

'I ain't leaving you here,' she wept. 'No fucking way.'

But Hastings was no longer listening. Knowles watched him slip away, his head slumping onto his left shoulder; the only movement was the snow as it settled upon him, covering him like a poignant shroud.

***

Within the blizzard, the war machine knelt down beside the inert human body, its large simian hands gently clearing away the snow. Johns was beyond death, his condition was no longer defined by the science of man. His bones had become jelly; his clothing and flesh were the same consistency. The alien commander used the machine's hands to scoop up saggy tissue. With one swift movement, Johns was folded and rolled into a macabre cylinder, a small vent opened in the side of the machine. As though stowing a sleeping bag, the alien put the Johns' remains into a storage compartment behind its combat chassis.

It closed the vent and was once more cocooned inside its machine. The tiny screen and the sparkling lights that danced before its cod-like eyes were sending it messages from a place many leagues from here, another base that they would take several days to reach given the power of the incoming storm. Their cargo was precious, the being that had once been Johns was transcending; soon it would become as great a weapon as their kind had ever known.

A weapon that would give them the means to win the war that was to come. A war that would see them become the new rulers of the world from which they had hidden away for centuries.

The commander signalled for his platoon to move out, and the army of hirsute warriors moved with determination across the snow, Arc-weapons poised and ready to strike down any threat.

The dull thud of rotor blades came from high above, and the platoon trained their weapons skywards. But the storm was too thick for Appleby's flight crew to risk a landing no matter how much money was at stake. They bailed after three attempts to navigate the storm, heading off west to Pokhara, ignorant as to how close they had come to being sent to oblivion.

As one line, the war machines moved through the blizzard, unimpeded and relentless. Only the token attempts of the blizzard between them and their destiny.

EPILOGUE

Knowles bowed her head and silently wept. All she had known was now gone, lost on the frozen slopes of a sacred mountain. Maybe the locals were right, and there was a curse here after all. The outcome had been the same. For an age, she had sought loneliness - they all had to some degree - but now it wasn't her bag, now it felt like the most terrible thing in the world.

She paused in her grief. It wasn't really the most terrible thing in the world, was it? No, that accolade went to the things now moving across the frozen landscape, the things that had brought so much pain and destruction to her life.

Knowles placed a hand on Hastings' chest and held it there for a few seconds; a final farewell before standing and going to Sully.

The great beast was staring out through the snow storm beyond the plane to an unseen horizon. The wind tousled his fur, clods of ice clung to his body. He had his head tilted back as his great snout flared and snorted in air and snow. As he sensed her next to him, he looked down, his head cocked to one side, and placed a big hand on her shoulder, an act of concern that she immediately understood. She patted the back of his mitt and nodded an understanding.

Knowles used her Arc Rifle to gesture to the fading tracks left behind by the platoon of war machines. Then she looked back up at her companion who was once again seeking out alien scent on the bitter wind.

'So,' she yelled up at him. 'Are we going to get those fuckers or what?'

END

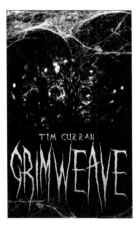

CHECK OUT OTHER GREAT HORROR NOVELS

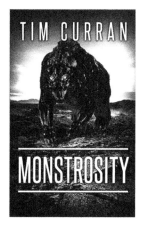

MONSTROSITY
by Tim Curran

The Food. It seeped from the ground, a living, gushing, teratogenic nightmare. It contaminated anything that ate it, causing nature to run wild with horrible mutations, creating massive monstrosities that roam the land destroying towns and cities, feeding on livestock and human beings and one another. Now Frank Bowman, an ordinary farmer with no military skills, must get his children to safety. And that will mean a trip through the contaminated zone of monsters, madmen, and The Food itself. Only a fool would attempt it. Or a man with a mission.

THE SQUIRMING
by Jack Hamlyn

You are their hosts.

You are their food.

The parasites came out of nowhere, squirming horrors that enslaved the human race. They turned the population into mindless pack animals, psychotic cannibalistic hordes whose only purpose was to feed them.

Now with the human race teetering at the edge of extinction, extermination teams are fighting back, killing off the parasites and their voracious hosts. Taking them out one by one in violent, bloody encounters.

The future of mankind is at stake.

And time is running out.

CHECK OUT OTHER GREAT HORROR NOVELS

DEATH CRAWLERS
by Gerry Griffiths

Worldwide, there are thought to be 8,000 species of centipede, of which, only 3,000 have been scientifically recorded. The venom of Scolopendra gigantea—the largest of the arthropod genus found in the Amazon rainforest—is so potent that it is fatal to small animals and toxic to humans. But when a cargo plane departs the Amazon region and crashes inside a national park in the United States, much larger and deadlier creatures escape the wreckage to roam wild, reproducing at an astounding rate. Entomologist, Frank Travis solicits small town sheriff Wanda Rafferty's help and together they investigate the crash site. But as a rash of gruesome deaths befalls the townsfolk of Prospect, Frank and Wanda will soon discover how vicious and cunning these new breed of predators can be. Meanwhile, Jake and Nora Carver, and another backpacking couple, are venturing up into the mountainous terrain of the park. If only they knew their fun-filled weekend is about to become a living nightmare.

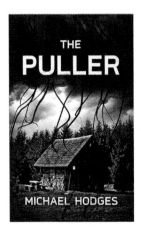

THE PULLER
by Michael Hodges

Matt Kearns has two choices: fight or hide. The creature in the orchard took the rest. Three days ago, he arrived at his favorite place in the world, a remote shack in Michigan's Upper Peninsula. The plan was to mourn his father's death and figure out his life. Now he's fighting for it. An invisible creature has him trapped. Every time Matt tries to flee, he's dragged backwards by an unseen force. Alone and with no hope of rescue, Matt must escape the Puller's reach. But how do you free yourself from something you cannot see?

Printed in Great Britain
by Amazon

79264905R00082